HEAVENLY
DATE

AND OTHER
FLIRTATIONS

HEAVENLY DATE

AND OTHER FLIRTATIONS

ALEXANDER McCALL SMITH

WHEELER

WINDSOR

PARAGON

This Large Print edition is published by Wheeler Publishing, Waterville, Maine USA and by BBC Audiobooks, Ltd, Bath, England.

Published in 2004 in the U.S. by arrangement with Canongate Books.

Published in 2004 in the U.K. by arrangement with Canongate Books Ltd.

U.S. Softcover 1-58724-764-X (Softcover)
U.K. Hardcover 1-4056-1000-X (Windsor Large Print)
U.K. Softcover 0-7540-6896-X (Paragon Large Print)

The text of this Large Print edition is unabridged.
Other aspects of the book may vary from the original edition.

Set in 16 pt. Plantin.

Printed in the United States on permanent paper.

British Library Cataloguing-in-Publication Data available

Library of Congress Cataloging-in-Publication Data

McCall Smith, Alexander, 1948–
    Heavenly date and other flirtations / Alexander McCall
    Smith.
    p. cm.
    Contents: Wonderful date — Nice little date — Bulawayo
— Far north — Intimate accounts — Calwarra — Fat date
— Maternal influence — Heavenly date.
    ISBN 1-58724-764-X (lg. print : sc : alk. paper)
    1. Dating (Social customs) — Fiction.   2. Humorous
stories, Scottish.   3. Large type books.   I. Title.
PR6063.C326H43 2004
   823'.914—dc22   2004052029

HEAVENLY DATE

AND OTHER FLIRTATIONS

CONTENTS

WONDERFUL DATE

Herr Brugli's bedroom was in the front of his mansion, looking out over the waters of the Lake of Zürich. In the early mornings he would stand in his dressing gown at the window, sipping a cup of milky coffee, while his valet ran his bath. The valet, Markus, was Polish, and had been with Herr Brugli for fifteen years. He knew the exact temperature which Herr Brugli preferred for his bath water; he knew the precise blend of coffee which his employer liked in the morning and the place on the breakfast table where Herr Brugli expected the morning's copy of *Die Neue Züricher Zeitung* to be awaiting him. Markus knew everything.

Markus knew, too, that Herr Brugli liked Madame Verloren van Thermaat, a Belgian lady who lived two miles away, also on the shores of the lake, also in a mansion. Verloren van Thermaat — what a ridiculous name, he thought. Madame Lost Tomato, that's what I call her!

"Should I marry Madame Thermaat?" Herr Brugli asked him one day, as he brought in the morning tray. "What are your views, Markus? You know me well enough by now. What do you think? Should a widower like myself marry a widow like Madame Thermaat? Do you think that that's what people expect of us?"

Markus laid his tray on the bedside table, exactly where Herr Brugli liked it to be laid. Then he crossed the room to open the curtains, glancing as he did so at his employer's face, reflected in the wardrobe mirror. Markus had to admit to himself that he was frightened. Everything about his job was to his liking. There was very little to do. He was paid handsomely by Herr Brugli, who never counted the bottles in his cellar, ever. He and his wife lived in a small cottage in the grounds, not more than a few paces from the private jetty. They had a small boat, which they liked to sail in the summer. Madame Thermaat might change all that. She had her own staff. She might edge them out.

"I really couldn't say, sir," he said, adding: "Marriage is not always a bed of roses, of course. Some people are happier by themselves."

He saw Herr Brugli smile.

"Anyway, perhaps I anticipate matters rather. Madame Thermaat is an independent person. Her life is very satisfactory at present."

Now Herr Brugli stood before the mirror in his dressing room and adjusted his tie. He was wearing his most comfortable suit, made, like all his suits, in London. Every year he went there for his wardrobe, ordering several suits and pairs of handmade shoes. Nobody made clothes like the English, he thought, which was rather surprising, bearing in mind what a scruffy group of people they were in general — young people in blue jeans with tears in the knees; men in shapeless, shiny jackets with zips in front; women in unflattering trousers and everyone, it seemed, in running shoes! And yet they made those wonderful clothes for other people — tweeds, cords, mohairs, checks, tartans.

This suit was just right for the occasion. It was made of a thick brown tweed, with a double-breasted waistcoat, and would keep him warm if the day turned nasty, although that looked unlikely, he thought; the sky was quite clear and there were signs of spring everywhere. It would be a perfect day.

He ate his breakfast slowly, perusing the columns of the newspaper, noting the obituaries — nobody today, thank God — finally turning to the stock reports. There was satisfactory news there, too. Everything was up on the previous day's trading, which is how it should be.

He laid aside the paper, wiped his mouth on the starched table napkin which Markus had patiently taught the Italian maid to iron in just the right way, and then he got up from the table. There was a short time to wait before the car would be at the door and he would set off. For a moment he was unsure what to do. He could write a letter, or read perhaps — he was half-way through *The Magic Mountain*, but he was out of sympathy with it for some reason. German literature was so depressing, he felt; so heavy and full of woe. What a bleak vision they have, our neighbours to the north; what a frightful group of people for the most part, terribly greedy. But they eat our chocolates, I suppose.

He went to his bureau and took out his writing case. There was a letter to be written to his cousin in Buenos Aires. She wrote to him once a month, and he always wrote back within three days of receiving her letter. She had nothing to do, of course, and her letters reflected this; but he was dutiful in family matters and since he had been left on his own the burden of correspondence had fallen on him.

"Dear Hetta: What a gorgeous day it is today — a real peach of a day. The lake is still, and there is no movement in the air. Yet spring is here, I can feel it, or almost here, and very soon we shall have blossom in the garden again! Alas, you will slide into autumn, and winter then, but I shall think of you as I sit in the garden."

He paused. She knew about Madame Thermaat, of course, but he did not want her to feel that there was any understanding which did not yet exist. Perhaps just a mention then: "Today I am accompanying Madame Thermaat — I have told you of her, of course — into Zürich. We are going to take a short walk by the river, as it is such a lovely day, and I have one or two matters to attend to. Then we shall come back." He wondered if he should say more, but decided that this was quite enough. Let them speculate in Buenos Aires if they liked.

Markus came in to tell him that the car was ready outside. He got up from his desk and walked into the hall. There was another mirror there, and he looked anxiously at his reflection. The tie needed straightening, but he was sure he was right about the suit — it was exactly what the day required.

"Good-bye Markus," he said. "I shall be back at the usual time."

Markus held the door open for him, and the driver, seeing him emerge, started the engine of the car. They moved out on to the road, into the traffic, and edged their way up the lake to collect Madame Thermaat.

"My dear Madame Thermaat!"
"Dear Herr Brugli!"
They beamed at one another.
"Would you like the rug across your knees? There's still a bit of a nip in the air, isn't there?"

She shook her head. "I am perfectly warm," she said. "I never feel the cold."

"You are so fortunate," he said. "I feel cold in summer."

"Thin blood," she said. "You must have thin blood."

He laughed. "I shall try to thicken it up. What do you recommend? Do any of those health magazines you read tell you how to do it?"

"Chocolate, Herr Brugli! Lots of chocolate!"

He wagged his finger at her in mock disapproval. They were well on their way to Zürich now, and the large, high-powered car shot past slower vehicles. He asked her what she had been doing, and she described her week. It had, she said, been trying: she had two meetings of the village board, and they had ended in an impasse on each occasion, which was worrying. And then she had had three bridge evenings — *three* — all of which meant that she had had no time to herself at all.

He nodded sympathetically. He had weeks like that himself.

"And you have your factories too," she said. "You have to worry about them."

"To an extent," he agreed. "But thank heavens for my managers."

The car turned over the Cathedral Bridge and into the heart of the city. At the end of Bahnhof Strasse it pulled in to the side and allowed them both to alight. He got out first and held the door open for his companion.

"Thank you dear Herr Brugli," she said. "Now, where shall we start?"

He wagged his finger at her again.

"You know very well," he scolded. "Sprungli's — as always!"

They crossed the street and walked a few yards to a large glass door on which in ornate gold script the name Sprungli's was embossed. They walked past a man sitting on a bench, whose eyes fixed on them as they went past. He muttered something, and held out a hand, but neither heard nor saw him.

The counters in Sprungli's were laden with bank upon bank of chocolates. He paused before a tray of Belgian chocolates, and examined them carefully. Her eye was caught by a cake, which was topped by a small icing-sugar swan.

"Such skilful sculpting," she said. "It seems a pity to eat such an exquisite little work of art."

"A trifle overdone," he said. "I prefer a simpler approach."

"Perhaps, Herr Brugli," she conceded. "Simplicity is certainly an ideal in life."

They passed upstairs, where the waitress recognised them and led them immediately to a table in the corner. She was particularly attentive to Herr Brugli, who addressed her as Maria and asked after her mother.

"Ah," said the waitress. "She takes great pleasure in everything still. When the weather gets a bit better she will ride up to Rapperswill on the steamer to visit her sister."

"Marvellous!" said Herr Brugli, and turning to Madame Thermaat: "Eighty one, almost eighty two! A positive advertisement for a healthy life, is she not Maria?"

"And schnapps," said the waitress. "She drinks two glasses of schnapps each day. One before breakfast, and one before retiring to bed."

"There you are!" exclaimed Herr Brugli. "You see!"

They looked at the menu, which was quite unnecessary, as Herr Brugli never chose anything new, and expected Madame Thermaat to do the same.

"I think we shall have our usual again," he said to the waitress.

A few minutes later Maria brought them their coffee, served in tall glasses with whipped cream floating on the top. Then a plate of cakes arrived, and they each chose two. Maria returned, topped up the coffee, and cleared the uneaten cakes away.

"Take those back to your mother," said Herr Brugli. "Charge them to us."

Maria beamed. "She loves cakes," she said. "She can't resist them!"

There were few people of note in Sprungli's. There were several tables of tourists

— a party of Italians and a table of sober, intimidated Americans. Herr Brugli's gaze passed over these tables quickly.

"Nobody's in this morning," he began to say. "I don't see a soul . . ."

He stopped. Yes, there was somebody, and he leaned over the table to whisper to Madame Thermaat.

"Would you credit it?" he said, his voice barely audible. "There she is, that Zolger woman with her young friend. In broad daylight . . ."

Madame Thermaat followed his gaze.

"Eating cakes!" she exclaimed. "Look, she's feeding him one with her fingers!"

Herr Brugli's eyes narrowed.

"He's young enough to be her son," he whispered. "Just look at that! Just look at the way she's gazing at him."

"Eyes for nothing else," said Madame Thermaat. "Positively devouring him, in public."

They looked away, thrilled by their discovery. It was wonderful to see something as shocking as that; it added a spice to the day to see a late middle-aged Zürich matron — a prominent banker's wife — with her young lover in public, in a chocolate shop! It really was astonishingly good fortune, and cheered them both up immensely.

They arose from their table. He left fifty francs for Maria, tucked under a plate, as he always did. Then, eyes averted from the Zolger table, they made their way out of Sprungli's and into the street. It was even warmer now, and the city was bathed in clear spring sunlight; somewhere, over by the river, a clock chimed.

It was gallery time now, so they crossed the river again, skirted round the cheap shops which ruined the arcade, and began to climb up one of the narrow streets that wound their way up the hill to the Church of St John. She walked beside him, on the inside, and when they negotiated a tricky corner she took his arm — which he liked — but released it later once the danger had passed.

The Gallery Fischer was discreet. It had a display window, but only a small one, and this tended to contain some item from Herr Fischer's private collection, and would have nothing to do with what was inside. The door was always locked, but there was a small bell, which said simply *Fischer* and this, if rung, produced a small, stout man wearing round wire-rimmed glasses.

"So, Herr Brugli . . . and Madame Verloren van . . . van . . ."

"Thermaat," said Herr Brugli. "Herr Fischer, you are well, I hope?"

"Everybody in Switzerland has a cold at the moment," said Herr Fischer. "But I do not. So I am grateful."

"There are so many germs around these days," said Madame Thermaat. "You just can't avoid them. They are everywhere."

Herr Fischer nodded his head sagely.

"I have great faith in Vitamin C," he said. "I take Vitamin C every day, without fail."

They followed him into a small room behind the gallery. A young woman in an elegant black trouser suit came out from an office, shook hands solemnly, and then went off to a cupboard in the corner of the office.

"Here it is, then," said Herr Fischer. "It is, I hope, what you had in mind."

He handed the figurine to Herr Brugli, who took it in both hands and held it up in front of him. For a few moments there was silence. Herr Brugli moved the figurine backwards and forwards, the better to examine it in the light.

"Yes," he said quietly. "This is absolutely perfect."

Herr Fischer showed his relief. "There are so few of them left," he said. "At least there are so few of them in this condition."

Herr Brugli passed the small porcelain figure to Madame Thermaat, who took it gingerly and examined it closely.

"Such lovely colours," she said. "So true to life."

She passed it back to Herr Fischer, who looked expectantly at Herr Brugli.

"I shall take it," said Herr Brugli. "If you could ask your man . . ."

"We shall deliver it with pleasure," said Herr Fischer.

Madame Thermaat had moved to the other side of the room and was looking at a small bronze on a table.

"Do you have anything — some small bibelot — which Madame Thermaat might like?" Herr Brugli asked Herr Fischer. "Some little present . . . ?"

Herr Fischer looked thoughtful. "There is something," he said. "A small egg, after Fabergé I'm afraid, not by him. But exquisite nonetheless."

Herr Brugli smiled. "She would like that." Then, very quietly: "The price?"

Herr Fischer lowered his voice. He did not like talking about money, even with somebody like Herr Brugli. "Eight thousand francs," he said. "An absolute snip. If it were by Fabergé himself, then, well . . ."

Herr Brugli was eager to save the proprietor embarrassment. "Perfectly reasonable," he said. "Could we see if she likes it?"

"Leave it up to me," Herr Fischer assured him. "I shall fetch it immediately." It was a minute egg, fashioned out of silver, with gold lining and encrustation. The top, which could be pushed back, was lined within with mother-of-pearl, and the rest of the egg's interior was covered with jet.

"I believe that this might have been a pill box," said Herr Fischer. "It is, I believe, of French manufacture."

Madame Thermaat took the tiny egg in her

hands and peered at it intensely.

"So delightful," she said. "So modest. I'll take it please."

Herr Fischer seemed momentarily perplexed. He looked at Herr Brugli, who waved a hand in the direction of the egg.

"I should like to buy that for Madame Thermaat," he said. "Put it in my account."

"But I intended to buy it myself," protested Madame Thermaat. "You're far too kind to me."

"It is a little present that I already planned to buy you," said Herr Brugli. "You were not meant to buy it yourself."

Herr Fischer brushed aside Madame Thermaat's objections and took the egg from her.

"I shall wrap it in gold foil," he said. "Afterwards, you may press the gold foil down on some special object and gild it."

Madame Thermaat's eye alighted on a small painting on one of the walls. A haloed figure appeared to be floating several feet above the ground, surrounded by admiring bystanders and several surprised animals.

"That is most intriguing," she said to Herr Fischer. "What is it?"

Herr Fischer took the painting down. "Joseph of Copertino. A remarkable figure. He levitated on over seventy occasions and flew quite considerable distances on others. That, I believe, is why he is the patron saint of air travellers."

"A charming painting," she said.

"Late seventeenth century, Florentine," he said, lowering his voice even further. "Remarkable value at nineteen thousand francs."

"Would Herr Brugli like it?" asked Madame Thermaat.

"He would love it," Herr Fischer whispered. "Between ourselves, I gather that he is just the *slightest* bit frightened of travelling by air. This painting will undoubtedly reassure him."

Madame Thermaat inclined her head slightly. "Will you send me the bill?" she said to Herr Fischer. "Madame Verloren van Thermaat."

"Of course," said Herr Fischer. "And Herr Brugli — is he to know about this?"

Madame Thermaat took the painting from Herr Fischer and handed it to Herr Brugli.

"A little gift from me," she said. "To thank you for all your kindness."

They left Herr Fischer's shop, each carrying the present which the other had bought. It had turned slightly colder now, although the sun was still shining brilliantly, and Herr Brugli turned up the collar of his coat. Madame Thermaat took his arm again, and together they made their way down the narrow streets, back towards the river.

They passed a coffee bar, popular with students, and the smell of freshly ground coffee wafted out to them.

"I could do with a coffee," said Herr Brugli. "What about you? Could you do with one too?"

Madame Thermaat could, and so they entered the coffee bar, both feeling a little bit excited at the prospect of a new place with new, younger people. Zürich had changed over the previous few years, and you were never quite sure whom you might meet. Parts of it were Bohemian now; parts were even dangerous. There were foreigners — Eastern Europeans and others — exotica, thought Herr Brugli.

They found a small table near the bar and a waitress came to serve them. She had black fish-net tights and looked somewhat dishevelled. She was wearing a cheap perfume that made Madame Thermaat wrinkle her nose.

Herr Brugli smiled, conspiratorially. "This is rather different, is it not?"

Madame Thermaat looked about her. "What do these people do?" she said to him, her voice lowered. "Do you think they actually study?"

Herr Brugli shrugged his shoulders. "Perhaps," he said. "They study at night — perhaps."

Their coffee arrived. It was piping hot and very strong.

"So welcome," said Herr Brugli. "In whatever surroundings."

He looked at his watch, and saw that it

was almost lunchtime. For a moment he was thoughtful; then he called the waitress across and whispered something to her. She muttered something, and returned later with a bottle of champagne, which Herr Brugli inspected. Then he nodded and said something further to the waitress. She appeared surprised, but smiled after a moment and disappeared behind the bar.

"You're conspiring Herr Brugli!" scolded Madame Thermaat. "You're planning some mischief!"

A few minutes later the waitress returned, accompanied by a man in an apron. He was carrying two magnums of champagne. He put the champagne down on the bar and then, to Madame Thermaat's astonishment, clapped his hands loudly. The conversation died down. People looked up from the tables; a woman laid down her cigarette; a young man, who was in the process of getting up from his chair, sat down again.

"Ladies and Gentlemen," said the man. "I am happy to announce that each table may, if it wishes, have a magnum of champagne, by courtesy of one of our honoured guests." He paused, his hand stretched out to introduce Herr Brugli.

One of the students laughed.

"Good for the honoured guest! Where's the champagne?"

The waitress opened the first bottle and

gave it to a table of young men. Then others received their bottle and the wine was poured.

"Herr Brugli!" said Madame Thermaat. "Such a generous gesture! I think the students approve."

They did. Glasses were raised from all quarters of the restaurant, and Herr Brugli and Madame Thermaat acknowledged the toasts. Herr Brugli himself had two large glasses of champagne and felt immediately exhilarated by the flinty wine.

"This really is proving to be a marvellous day," he said expansively. "Such wonderful weather — such wonderful company!"

Madame Thermaat smiled demurely, raising her glass to her lips. She was more moderate in her consumption of champagne, but enjoyed it nonetheless. The students, of course, drank quickly. Soon the first magnums had been exhausted, but a sign from Herr Brugli to the waitress produced more. The man in the apron looked dubious, but money changed hands and he went away smiling.

Glasses refreshed, the students' conversation became more animated. At one table there was uproarious laughter; at another an earnest debate; at yet another, a student broke into a snatch of song.

A couple of students now got up and came over to the table at which Herr Brugli and Madame Thermaat were sitting. They were a boy and a girl — in their late teens or very early twenties by the look of them — dressed in the uniform of the student quarter, jeans and black jackets.

"May we join you?" asked the boy. "It was very kind of you to give us all champagne."

Herr Brugli rose to his feet, drawing up a chair for the girl.

"Of course," he said. "It has been a very great pleasure to see you all enjoying yourselves so much. It's just like *The Student Prince* . . ."

The students looked blank.

"Surely you remember the film," interjected Madame Thermaat. "Mario Lanza was the prince. He was a student too . . ."

The girl shook her head. "An old film?" she asked.

Madame Thermaat laughed. "Goodness!" she said. "I suppose we forget just how old we are. Yes, I suppose it was an old film."

"We saw *Casablanca* last week," offered the boy. "It was terribly good. It was at a festival of historic films."

Herr Brugli glanced at Madame Thermaat. "It was a truly great film," he said. "It was probably the best film ever made. I saw it shortly after it came out," adding: "Although I was terribly young at the time, just a boy really."

There was a short silence. Herr Brugli reached for his bottle of champagne and filled up the students' glasses.

"Tell us all about yourselves," he said. "Tell us what you study. Tell us where you live. Tell us which professors are worth listening to and which are not."

They walked out of the coffee house together. The boy took Madame Thermaat's arm, for which she was grateful, after four glasses of champagne — and Herr Brugli took the girl's.

"Our place is just a minute or two away," said the boy. "It's nothing much, I'm afraid."

"What does one need in life?" asked Herr Brugli. "A glass of wine, a book, a bough, and thou? Is that not what Omar Khyham says."

"Yes," said the boy, hesitantly. "Maybe . . ."

They passed a bookshop and then followed a narrow lane that led back up the hill. Then there was an alley, with several bicycles propped against the walls, and graffiti daubed on the plaster. There was a slightly dank smell in the air, an odour of cats, thought Herr Brugli.

"Here we are," said the girl. "This door to the right."

They entered the doorway. There was a cramped hall, and a set of narrow stone stairs which the boy bounded up. From a landing above, he called down to them: "Door's open! Up you come!"

Madame Thermaat went in first, followed

by the girl. Then Herr Brugli entered, stooping under the squat lintel of the door, holding his felt hat in one hand and his parcel in the other.

There were only two rooms. One was a living room, neatly kept, but sparsely furnished. There were several large cushions on the floor and a sofa covered with a tartan rug. There were posters on the wall — a picture of a man's head, a travel poster from Greece, an Italian railway timetable. There were books stacked in a narrow bookcase and several forming a pile on the floor itself.

The door into the other room was open, and they could see a large mattress on the floor. Beside the mattress there was a vase of dried flowers and more books. Herr Brugli averted his gaze, guilty, awed.

"You see," said the boy. "This is how we live. This is our place."

"It's charming," said Madame Thermaat. "And look, you can see the Cathedral down there!"

Herr Brugli joined her at the window and they looked down at the roof tops of the city, falling away below them towards the river. It was a view of the city they were unused to; it could even have been another town.

"I would like to live somewhere like this," said Herr Brugli quietly. "Away from everything. Just by oneself. Imagine it."

Madame Thermaat closed her eyes. "You

wouldn't have to worry about anything," she murmured. "No staff troubles. No bridge parties. No telephone."

"It would be blissful," said Herr Brugli. "Heaven."

The girl had switched some music on — it was jazz, a saxophonist — while the boy ground coffee.

"Listen," said Herr Brugli, raising a finger in the air. "You know what that is, don't you. *As time goes by*! *Casablanca*!"

He turned to Madame Thermaat.

"We should dance," he said. "Would you care to?"

"I should love to," she replied.

The boy set the mugs of coffee down on a low table. Then he went to the girl and took her by the hand. They danced too, next to Herr Brugli and Madame Thermaat. *As time goes by* finished, and now it was *Afternoon in Paris*; only Herr Brugli knew what that was, but they all danced again. Then the boy danced with Madame Thermaat, and Herr Brugli danced with the girl.

Now the boy opened a bottle of wine — cheap Swiss wine from up the lake — but Herr Brugli said it was the most delicious wine he had had for many years. Madame Thermaat agreed, and drank two glasses.

Suddenly Herr Brugli looked at his watch.

"Look at the time!" he said. "Almost five o'clock!"

"We must be on our way," said Madame Thermaat. "I have so much to do."

"And so do I," said Herr Brugli.

The boy said he was sorry they were leaving. They could have had dinner in the flat.

"Some other day," said Herr Brugli. "And perhaps some time you would both join us for dinner in our houses."

"That would be very nice," said the girl.

Herr Brugli looked at the girl. She was enchanting; kind, loving, wonderful — just wonderful. And the boy was so courteous too; nothing had really changed in Switzerland, nothing. He leant over to Madame Thermaat and whispered in her ear. She listened gravely, and then nodded enthusiastically.

"We are so grateful to you for your kindness," said Herr Brugli. "Asking us home, and arranging this impromptu little dance — everything. We have presents for you, and you must accept them."

He passed the painting to the boy, and Madame Thermaat pressed the jewelled egg, in its wrapping of gold foil, into the girl's hands.

The boy looked embarrassed as he took the paper off the parcel. He was silent as he studied the painting, holding it tenderly.

"It's marvellous," he said. "It looks just like an original. It's so realistic."

Herr Brugli laughed. "But it is the original,"

he said. "It's Florentine."

"And the egg is French, not Russian," said Madame Thermaat. "Not, alas, by Fabergé, but by a follower."

The girl looked mutely at the boy, who raised an eyebrow.

"These presents are too generous," he said. "It's very kind of you, but we can't . . . we can't accept them."

"But of course you can," said Herr Brugli. "You would offend us if you did not. Is that not so, Madame Thermaat?"

"Yes," she said. "It is."

They bade farewell at the end of the lane. The boy and girl stood there for a few minutes, his arm around her waist, and at the bottom of the hill Herr Brugli turned round to wave to them. Then a taxi stopped and he ushered Madame Thermaat into it.

He gave the address, and they set off in the direction of the lake road.

"What a wonderful day it has been," sighed Herr Brugli. "We've done so very much."

"Our days in Zürich are always wonderful," said Madame Thermaat.

"Next Wednesday then," said Herr Brugli. "Shall we go out again?"

"Yes," said Madame Thermaat. "That would be very suitable. Perhaps we'll have good weather again."

The taxi drove on. They sat in silence now,

each separately reflecting on the satisfaction of the day. They passed blocks of flats, garages, parks. Now they were going through an industrial area, and there were factories. One stood out — with a great blue sign in neon light, illuminated against the dark of the sky — *Brugli's Chocolate*. But Herr Brugli did not see it, as his eyes were closed in sheer pleasure and from the fatigue that comes from a busy day. Madame Thermaat was looking out over the lake. She would play bridge later that night, with her friends, as usual. She had had a bad hand of cards last time, but she was completely confident that tonight they would be decidedly better.

NICE LITTLE DATE

They treated him well — as he found they always did in hotels which had aspirations for just one more elusive star.

"We've reserved your usual room," the manager had said, pleased with himself at having remembered. "The one you had last year. The one which looks out over the trees. I believe you liked it."

"I did like it. Yes."

He had smiled, and thanked them. It gave him a feeling of security, to be known, at least to them. They understood, as well; they were discreet, when necessary. There had never been any trouble with them, any embarrassment over anything.

Now he handed them the key as he went out for the evening, and the clerk tucked it away under the desk.

"It's a splendid evening," he said. "It's going to become cooler. A good evening to go out walking. To see the city."

"Yes," he had said, and then walked out through the revolving door into the scented heat of the front garden, with its flowering trees and shrubs. The air was heavy, and it embraced him like the waters of a tepid bath;

a little bit too hot, he thought, but it would cool down shortly, once the sun disappeared.

He left the hotel gardens and followed the road that wound its way down the hill, down towards the heart of the city. He had made no plans for the evening, but in the back of his mind he knew what was going to happen. It was best, though, not to acknowledge it, but to wait and see. One could never tell how things were going to work out. There might be nobody. His courage might fail him. He might think better of it, change his mind — return to the hotel and go back to his room to read. That happened more often than not.

The road began to drop steeply, winding past houses and cramped gardens, past shuttered shops, a convent, a church. People passed him, carrying the evening's shopping, wheeling bicycles. An old man watched him from his doorway, and he acknowledged him courteously in Portuguese. The old man nodded, closing his rheumy eyes and then re-opening them. For a moment he thought he might stop, to say something, to ask him about the neighbourhood, but a girl had approached the old man from behind and was tugging urgently on his shirtsleeve.

He stopped for a few moments outside some of the shop windows and looked inside. It seemed to have become a quarter of antique shops and book dealers. There was a window display of faded editions of Pessoa, with a picture of the poet in the middle, surrounded by the works of his various *personae*, Alberto Camos, Ricardo Reis, Fernando Soares. It had always astonished him that somebody could write so differently, depending on whose name would appear on the work. Today they would treat him as ill, as a multiple personality; there would be critics who would write like doctors; they would make it a clinical matter, and kill the poetry stone dead in the process.

There was a shop which sold memorabilia of the Empire in Africa, discreetly, almost apologetically. Nobody spoke about it any more, about the vast, nightmare colonies; but they must be there in the city, retired officials who had spent their working lives in distant towns in Mozambique and Angola, and who had come back to a country that wanted nothing more than to erase its memory. They could hardly forget, though; they could hardly be expected to cancel out those years altogether; they could hardly pretend that they had been doing nothing very much for twenty, thirty years of overseas service. They must talk about it sometimes at least, even if only among themselves, furtively, like criminals discussing their crimes.

Perhaps this was their shop, where they could come and find the familiar atlases, the dog-eared administrative manuals churned out by the Colonial Institute, the grammars of the minor languages. All that effort, that striving; and all that it led to — debts, death, ignominy. He looked through the window more closely. Most of it should be discarded; the ribbons of old medals, a carved walking stick of African hardwood, a soapstone head. His eye was caught by an ancient tin first aid kit, with a name stencilled on the lid. It would have been thrown out a few years ago — nobody could possibly have wanted to buy it — but now it appeared to have some sort of value. Perhaps it would trigger a memory somewhere, or make one for somebody who didn't remember it at all, who was not even born when Salazar fell.

There was somebody beside him at the window, looking through the dust at the objects in the window.

"They're asking us back," he said. "They're asking us back to run their farms. Can you believe it? After all that happened. The war, Frelimo, the dispossessions, the lot. The Marxists asking us back!"

He looked at his companion, who smiled at him, almost conspiratorially, revealing several gold teeth.

He tried to think what to say, but nothing came to mind.

"I never thought I'd see that day, I can tell you!" the other man said. "But there you have it. You can never tell what's going to happen. Never."

He nodded in agreement, and the other man walked off, chuckling at his observation.

Then he knew what he wanted to say, what he should have said. You shouldn't try to forget your past. There's no point in denial. Confront it, as the Germans do; worry away at it, dissect it, let it haunt you, until you can look at it. Which you can, eventually.

He reached the square, and went into a small bar. He ordered a coffee, a strong one, and then a glass of port. The proprietor served him, and then returned to his newspaper. There was a political crisis, and the lurching of a government was blazoned across the page. He found their politics impenetrable, as the politics of others so frequently are, and he did not try to understand.

The proprietor put down the newspaper.

"Disgusting," he said.

"Yes."

There was a brief silence.

"You're not local?"

"No. I come from America. From South Carolina."

"Your Portuguese is good. Usually Americans . . ."

He smiled, and interrupted. "Don't bother to learn."

The proprietor looked apologetic. "Perhaps some of them do. You have."

"I worked in Brazil. For years. You'll probably

37

notice it in my accent."

The proprietor nodded. "One can always tell."

He asked for another glass of port, which he drank quickly, although it was still too warm and he should have been drinking *vinho verde*. Perhaps later.

He thanked the proprietor and went out into the square. It was now quite dark, and the lights were on in the gardens in the centre of the square, pools of yellow along the pathways. He crossed the road and went into the gardens, where there were benches. His heart was beating more quickly now, and his mouth felt dry. He never got used to it; never became brazen; never.

He picked a bench which had been placed directly above an elaborate mosaic — a picture of a ship on the waves with dolphins cavorting about the bow. There was an inscription too, a line of poetry, but some of the letters had gone missing, and he could not make sense of it. Something about the heart.

He sat there for fifteen minutes or so, watching. The square was becoming busier now, and there was the smell of cooking from doorways. There was music somewhere, snatches of it, and he felt calmer. He loved this city, with all its clutter and its beauty, and its handsome people. It was his favourite place for . . . for what I like to do, he said to himself. It's not wrong. It's tolerated here, just, even if at home the puritans would take a different view.

Somebody walked past his bench, went on a short distance, and then returned to sit down beside him.

"Do you have a light for my cigarette?" the other said, taking a packet of cheap cigarettes out of his coat pocket.

He shook his head.

"I'm sorry. I don't smoke."

"Ah well," said the man. "It would do me good. It's an effort to give up the things one enjoys, don't you think?" He paused. "And the things *you* enjoy? Would you like to give them up?"

He looked down at the mosaic.

"No. I have no plans to give them up."

The man took a cigarette out of the pack and then reached into his pocket for a lighter.

"Can I help you in some way?" he said. "You're obviously a stranger. It's a long way from Brazil, isn't it?"

For a moment or two he said nothing, then he nodded.

The man drew on his cigarette. "I can arrange things for you. A boy?"

"No."

"You just tell me what you want then. Then come back in half an hour. The other side of the square. You give the money to me."

He told him, and the man nodded.

"I'll fix you up. A nice little date. Nice. Willing."

He watched for a minute or so before he crossed the square. The man had returned, but he was alone. That was just as it should be, so he walked across to join him.

"Follow me," said the man. "We're just going to go up that street over there."

He hesitated, which brought an assurance: "You can trust me, don't worry. There are plenty of people about. I'm not going to rob you."

"All right. But I don't want to go inside."

"You don't need to. She'll be waiting. But you pay me before you go off, understand?"

He followed him, and they made their way up the street until suddenly the man stopped and stepped back into a doorway.

"This is your friend, right here. See her? All right?"

He hardly looked at her. "How old?"

"Fourteen," said the man. "Just. She was still thirteen two weeks ago. It's respectable. You could marry her if you want."

The man laughed, watching his client's expression. He's a Protestant, he thought; the Americans are all Protestants and they feel guilt, even when they're going with a woman. What about the ones who went with boys, how did they feel? He had had a client, a rich man from Austin, who had apologised to him when he asked for a boy. *I'm not going to do anything to him, he said. I'm only going to ask him to . . . to . . . I like women too, you see. I only see boys now and then.* There had been a whole litany of excuses.

He passed over the money, and the girl watched as the notes were counted.

"Good. That's fine. She'll go with you to your hotel. You can have her until tomorrow morning. If you want to give her some extra money, you can. She'll find her own way back."

They walked away, the girl beside him. He had still hardly glanced at her, but he noticed that she was smiling at him.

"Would you like something to eat? Would you like to go to a restaurant?"

It was an unusual idea, even dangerous, but he had missed his lunch and was hungry. And, after all, the other man, the procurer, had described this as a date. He would take his date, this delectable little honey-coloured creature, out for a meal. He would treat her like a woman. Candlelight; compliments.

She looked up at him.

"If you want to."

"But would you like it? I'm asking you."

She shrugged. "I suppose so."

"You suppose so . . ." He stopped. Two weeks ago she had been thirteen; that's how they spoke.

★ ★ ★

He chose the first restaurant they passed, a large fish restaurant with an art nouveau front. A waiter standing at the door ushered him and showed him to a table with a flourish. It was an expensive place; thick, freshly-starched white linen, and rows of glasses at each place.

"Would you care for wine, sir?" the waiter passed him the list and then looked at the girl. "And for your daughter . . ."

He sat impassive, but the words cut at him, and cut. She had not noticed; she was just looking at the knives and forks and the glittering plates.

He ordered both for himself and for her, as he knew it would take too long to find out what she really wanted. They would have a sea-food platter, he said, with salads. The waiter wrote down the order, and disappeared.

"You're fourteen."

The girl nodded.

"And you live in Lisbon? You come from Lisbon?"

She lowered her eyes.

"I come from somewhere else. A place in the country. Now I live in the city."

"You live with that man? The one who . . . who introduced us?"

She shook her head. "I live with an aunt. She looks after me."

He studied her face. She had that olive

42

skin that he loved, but there was something odd, almost boyish, about her; she looked as if she could look after herself. This was not exploitation. She was tough enough. And they liked it, these kids. They were volunteers.

Suddenly the girl spoke.

"My aunt lived in Africa for years. In a place called Lourenço Marques. Do you know that place?"

He picked up a knife from the table and examined it. "Yes. I know that place. I've been there before."

The girl seemed interested now. "I really want to go there one day. I want to see the house my aunt lived in. She had a bar there, a big one, with servants."

"Yes, she would have had all that. I can imagine."

"And she used to swim in the Indian Ocean. Every morning."

"Dangerous. Sharks."

The girl looked surprised. "In the ocean? Sharks?"

"Yes. There are sharks."

She looked disappointed. An illusion had been shattered perhaps.

"But don't worry about it. It's only dangerous if you go out too far. The sharks wait out where the surf starts. You'd be safe near the beach."

The conversation dried up, and he was glad that the waiter had returned.

"For you sir, here, and for your daughter . . . there. *Bom appetito!*"

Back at the hotel it was the same clerk on duty. He asked for his key, watching the cool eyes of the clerk move to the girl, and then come back to him. He reached forward and slipped the bank note over the desk.

"It's cool outside now. Quite cool."

The clerk took the note, tactfully, and smiled as he handed over the key.

"Good night, sir. Thank you. Yes it is cool, quite cool."

He crossed the room to close the blinds. As he did so he looked out over the trees, the trees they knew he liked. There was a slight breeze, and the tops of the trees moved in response. Where do the winds come from? The winds that come from somewhere . . . A line of poetry he had read, a long time ago, in some forgotten book, in another country.

He turned round. The girl was standing beside the bed now, looking at him, and he saw again her eyes, almond-shaped, and the smoothness of her skin. He crossed over to her and held her shoulders lightly.

"I'm going to take your clothes off," he said. "All your clothes, starting with these."

He slipped his hand under the band of her jeans, and he felt her tense up.

"Are you frightened?"

She said nothing, and so he continued, fumbling with the zip, which he released and brought down. Then he pulled at the denim, and the jeans were at her feet. She had long legs for a girl; for a girl . . .

"Take the rest off," he said. "I'm going into the bathroom for a moment."

When he returned she was lying face down upon the bed, naked. He noticed the tiny ridge of the spine, the blades of the shoulder, the olive skin like a map of temptation.

"Turn over," he said. "Turn over."

She turned over, and looked at him, afraid of his reaction, ashamed.

He said nothing for a moment; he could not speak. Then, quietly: "You're a boy."

The boy said nothing. He sat up, crouching his legs, his head sunk between his knees.

"He makes me," he said. "It's him. He takes all the money." He looked up. "I promise you. He makes me go with men who want to go with boys. He also tricks men who want girls. They never dare complain."

He stared down at the boy, silent with pity.

"But you do live with your aunt?" he asked at last. "The one who lived in Africa? That's all true?"

The boy nodded. "Yes. She's his friend."

"I see."

He looked down at the boy. He was too thin. He needed to put on weight.

"You need to eat more," he said. "You should have proper meals. You're not eating the right things."

The boy looked up at him.

"How do you know?' he asked.

"Because I'm a doctor," he said.

BULAWAYO

Southern Rhodesia 1959

"There," she said. "There it is. Over there. Can you see it now?"

He looked in the direction in which she was pointing. There was a patch of dark green and, intermixed with it, half-concealed by vegetation and distance, he could make out smudges of white, the buildings. Behind the green, a background turbulence of rounded granite boulders pushed up from the veldt.

"By the trees?" he asked. "By the gum trees?"

She nodded. "Yes. That's it."

He smiled. "It's a good place for it to be. It looks as if there's plenty of water."

"It's always been green here. When there was that awful drought — you remember, five, six years ago . . ."

"Six," he interrupted. "The year I went overseas."

"Yes, I suppose it was. Anyway, we had bags of water then. They were talking about water rationing in Bulawayo. All the gardens were bone dry. Dead."

He swerved to avoid a rock which had

somehow been exposed in the middle of the dirt road.

"Close shave," he said. "I saw it just in time."

"What?"

"That rock. I lost a sump once down near Gwanda on one of those. There was oil all over the place."

She turned round in her seat and looked into the cloud of dust thrown up behind the car.

"I'll get my father to flatten it out. He's got one of those grading ploughs."

He grunted. "Good idea. But you take out one rock and there's another beneath it. A Landrover's the only answer. Does your old man drive one?"

"Yes."

They travelled in silence for a few minutes. Ahead of them, the road began to swing round towards the vlei where they had seen the green paddocks and the stand of trees. The farmhouse could now be made out — the white colonnades of a verandah, a thatched roof, a red flash of bougainvillaea. The road was smoother now and he accelerated for the last few miles of the journey. He liked to sweep up to houses and brake sharply in front of the verandah. Everybody did it out in the country, and it had always seemed to him to be a decisive way to arrive. And he needed to be decisive today, with this meeting ahead of him. A beer would go down well. Two or three perhaps. Dutch courage, that's what they called it. And why not?

Now, with her parents on the verandah, slyly looking at one another, though affecting not to, he took in every detail. She looks older than he is, he thought. But that's not unusual with farmers' wives. Somehow the weather seems to get to their faces before it does to the men's; they become pinched, leathery, like the faces of Australian women who have lived in the outback all their lives, but not so bad. Was it the children, the worry of running a home, childbirth, sex . . . Could there still be passion in that dried out frame, so primly dressed in its thin cotton print dress? And as for him, heavy-limbed and ponderous. Surely not.

"Michael?" He looked at her. She had asked him something.

"Would you like a cup of tea, then? Mother was wondering?"

He looked at her expectantly. "What about you?"

"Or a beer?" Her father spoke now, smiling. "It's hot enough."

He accepted with relief and sat down with her father as the two women went into the house. There was silence for a few moments. Yes, it was going to be awkward, although the beer would make it better.

"You're a teacher, Anne tells me. Mathematics?"

The voice was unusual for a farmer — unaccented, quiet. It was more like his own father's voice, a cautious, judicial voice. He remembered her telling him that he was a graduate of Cape Town, that he had studied something unlikely — archaeology?

"Yes. Mathematics, and a lot of physical education. I've been there two years now."

The older man smiled and nodded his head, as if some suspicion had been confirmed.

"I was a governor of the school once."

This came as a surprise. She had said nothing about that; but she had spoken very little about them. She had been interested in his family, and had quizzed him about his relatives, but it was as if there was nothing interesting about her own.

He reached for his beer and poured it into a tall glass.

"That was some years ago now. Our son, the one we lost, he was there, you know."

He had been told about that. She had referred to her dead brother in a manner of fact way, just as her father now spoke of him. He had no close family any more, so he couldn't tell, but he had always imagined that families stopped speaking of the dead, the intimate dead at least; that to do otherwise would resurrect the pain. He felt embarrassed by this. What could you say about another's dead son?

But there was no need: "I liked that school the first time I saw it. It seemed to have a good atmosphere about it. Do you feel that too, working there?"

"I do."

"What gives it that? What do you think?"

He had never really thought about it. He liked the place, but had never analysed why. He was happy there, and that was all there was to it.

"Good staff, I suppose." As he spoke, he realised that he sounded trite. There was an intelligence in the older man which he instinctively felt he couldn't match. He's shrewd, he thought; this farmer sitting here in the middle of all his cattle is cleverer than I am.

"Of course," her father said. "One or two people can set the tone for a place, can't they?" He paused. "And tradition, too. That's worth remembering, even these days."

"Of course."

"They tell me that it's old-fashioned to talk about tradition. A tabu word. What do you think of that?"

He felt irritated. What did he think? Did he think about that at all? His host was looking at him quizzically.

"I still believe in tradition," said the older man. "To an extent. I know there's a lot of nonsense in it, but without it, well, we'd just be adrift. It gives our lives a bit of . . . a bit of focus."

He was expecting an answer, or at least some comment. Tradition?

"They believe in it, don't they?" He pointed to the stables beyond the lawn. Two men were leading horses out into the pad-docks; two men clad in patched blue overalls and wearing fragments of discarded hats, hardly hats any longer. Her father laughed.

"The Africans? Yes. It's very important to them. Very important. They're superstitious though, aren't they. Do you think there's a difference?"

He reached for the beer that had quietly been placed before him on the mukwa-wood table and then answered his own question: "Probably."

The men who had been leading the horses into the paddock had stopped. One of them had run a hand down the foreleg of his horse and lifted the hoof to examine it. Then he loosened the halter and smacked the horse on the side of its neck. The other released his horse too and shouted. The horses shied away and cantered off.

"There they go," he said. "The two best horses in the place."

The young man watched the horses as they moved through the knee-high brown grass of the undergrazed paddock. It would be simpler, he thought, not to get involved in all this. He could remain unmarried and live in staff quarters for the rest of his life. Didn't that seem more natural for him, anyway? Did he really want to get married? He looked sideways at her father, the words running through his mind — father-in-law, father-in-law. It sounded strange and inappropriate. He would never be able to call him that. Other people had fathers-in-law; other people had wives.

"He's terribly good-looking. We like him. I could tell that your father liked him too. I sensed that immediately."

Her mother glanced at her, and saw that she was blushing.

"I never thought that you'd bring back anybody unsuitable. I never thought that for a moment."

There was a silence between them. The daughter looked down at the floor, absorbed in the pattern of the mat at her feet.

"When can we tell people?" her mother asked. "I hope we don't have to wait."

Now she spoke. "Any time. You can tell them any time now."

"That's good."

Neither said anything for the moment. Outside, they heard the sound of the diesel generator in the night. Her mother got up from her chair and went across to the window. There was nothing to see outside but the blackness of the night and the square of light from the window.

"It's so hot," she said. "There are times I wish we lived in the Cape or in the Eastern Highlands. Anywhere but Matabeleland."

"We'd like to get married in about six months' time," she said, to her mother's back.

"That would be fine. That would give you plenty of time to get things organised. There's always so much to do."

"We thought that the cathedral in Bulawayo . . ."

"Would be just right. Of course it would. There shouldn't be any problems. We can phone them in the morning."

Her mother turned round.

"My dear, I don't know how one puts these things these days, with everything being so different. People have different views nowadays . . ."

She paused. The daughter looked at her mother, and noticed that the hem of the faded dress has come down at one side.

"You see, in my day we really were expected to wait . . . you know, one didn't really allow men . . . But then, things were different when you became engaged. More was allowed then."

The daughter said nothing, silently willing her mother to stop speaking, but the older woman continued.

"Engaged couples have a certain leeway. But please, my dear, be careful. That's all I want to say. Remember that sometimes things can go wrong and then . . . Well, then, things may have gone further than you'd want and you may regret later . . ."

"Not being able to wear white after all, next time round?"

The mother smiled, the tension broken.

"Precisely," she said. "Precisely."

When he was eleven, his mother had left. He knew his parents argued; he had heard the raised voices and seen the tension on their faces when they were together, but he had assumed that this was how people lived. He knew that there were fights in other people's houses, that other parents were at each other's throats, and he knew that there was something called divorce, which happened to other families and which led to complications of two houses and two cars and split weekends. But when she left, suddenly, driving away after no more than a tense, silent good-night kiss, he was unprepared.

His father had come into his room to wake him one morning, and stood there, uneasily, his dressing gown draped around his shoulders.

"I've got sad news for you, Michael," he had begun. "Your mother's left us."

He had lain quite still, staring at the ceiling, unsure whether to pretend to be asleep, to shut the information out. But his father had stood there, staring at him, and he had had to answer.

"When will she come back?" he had asked.

"She isn't coming back, I'm afraid. She's gone to live with somebody else. They've gone to live up north, in Nairobi. I'm sorry."

And that had been all that had been said. They never talked about it again; he, sensing his father's pain, had kept off the subject; his father, feeling embarrassed and incapable of confronting his son's emotions, had simply pretended that nothing untoward had happened.

The running of the household presented no problems. The African housekeeper did the shopping and supervised the two maids. Everything worked. Clothes were washed and neatly ironed, shoes cleaned, and beds made. He never questioned it; it just happened.

His father, an attorney, spent all day in his office, but was always back at suppertime and never went out at night. At weekends, he took his son swimming, or into the hills to the south of the town, where they made breakfast fires and fried up sausages and bacon. When school holidays came round, he took him fishing on the Zambesi, an adventure which they both looked forward to for months before the event.

And so he grew up in a home which others, who knew of the adultery and the departure of his mother, described as "sad" or "pathetic", but which was secure enough for him.

Then, at seventeen, he returned one afternoon from a rugby match and found a blue and white police car parked in the drive. A neighbour was standing in front of the house; he stared at him, and then came walking briskly across the lawn to meet him.

His father, he was told, had been in an accident. He was seriously hurt, no it was worse; he was sorry, but he had to tell him this, there was nothing they could do for him. In fact, he had been killed. They were very sorry.

The other driver had been drunk. He was a railwayman, who had been drinking all morning at the railway social club and had careered down Rhodes Street, skipping the lights. He had knocked a street pedlar off his bicycle and had then met his father head-on at an intersection. The drunk was unhurt.

He heard nothing more. The following days were spent in numbness; he sat in the church, on the hard pew, and kept his eyes down, as if by sheer will power he might transport himself elsewhere, away from this. His father's partner sat next to him, and touched him gently on the sleeve when it was time to stand up. He did not look at the coffin, which he simply did not see, but he smelled the flowers, the sickly odour of the arum lilies, and he heard the words:

"This man, who was our brother in Christ, was a good man, a just man, who had disappointments in his life but who took them bravely. Some of you here, myself included, served alongside him in the Western Desert, and we remember the comradeship of those days. Each of us has his memories of an honourable man, who never stinted with his help. That is how a life should be led; with truth to friends, and loyalty to country, and kindness to the weak. Let us look to his example."

His father had been the adviser of a mission on the southern edge of the town, and the priests had urged that he should be buried there. So they drove out, in melancholy convoy, past the tennis courts of the country club, past the first huts of the farm servants, to the mission and its rickety-walled burial ground. It was midday, and hot, and a wind had arisen, making small clouds of red dust from the hard earth. He closed his eyes, but he had been there before, when his father had taken him to see the graves of the early missionaries.

There was one grave, with a stone which now listed badly, but which still stood to proclaim its message: CHARLES HELM, MISSIONARY, A FRIEND OF THE MATABELE. Now he opened his eyes again and stared at this stone, while to his side, across a gulf of empty painfulness, they buried his father.

The echoing resonances of the phrases

seemed to reach up to the empty white sky above them. *Man that is born of woman has but a short time to live . . . In the sure and certain hope of resurrection and in the life of the world to come.* Then silence, and the choir from the mission church, who had robed in white for the occasion, sang "God bless Africa".

He had been on the point of leaving school, so his father's partner, who had been appointed his trustee, decided that it was best for him to stay with them until his examinations were over. There was no shortage of funds; he could go to the university of his choice, and study what he wished. His father had been at Cambridge, and it was thought that this was the best place for him. He could go to his father's old college, which is what his father would have wanted; and it was a good place for mathematics, which is the subject he shone in.

"I'm not sure how I'll find England," he had said to the trustee. "I've never been there."

"You'll be as happy as a sandboy. Think of it! Living in a place like Cambridge. All the cricket and rugby you want. Wonderful buildings, friends, stimulation for the mind. Those wonderful English pubs. My God, if I were in your shoes!"

At first, Cambridge seemed cold to him,

alien and unfriendly, and he pined, sick at heart, for Africa. The skies were low, unlike the skies at home, as if there was not enough air, enough space. There were people all around him, but he was lonelier than he had ever been before. There were cousins of his father's, who lived in Norfolk, and they invited him for weekends, but he found them distant, though probably unintentionally so, and he was uncomfortable in their presence.

He had nobody to write to, except his trustee. He had told his mother of his departure, and there had been a telephone call, but her voice had been strained. He imagined that she felt guilty, and he, in turn, felt little for her.

He fell in with others who were in a position similar to his. There were a couple of Australians and a girl from New Zealand. They went to pubs together on Friday evenings, and made the occasional journey into London, to wander around the West End. Then slowly, they branched out and made other friends.

He found that he was popular. Women liked him for his looks — he turned heads, and knew it, but this seemed to mean nothing to him. He was invited to college dances, and went, but rarely returned the invitations he received.

"I can't make you out, Michael," commented one of his neighbours in college. "You don't seem to care about others very much, do you?"

60

He looked surprised. Of course he cared, as everybody did.

"You ignore all these girls who are throwing themselves — yes, throwing themselves — at your feet. You could have any number of them, you know. A different girl every week. Every night, if you really set to it."

He smiled. "That wouldn't leave much time, would it? For other things."

His friend stared at him. "You like girls, I take it?"

He was surprised. "Yes. I like them."

"Are you sure?"

He nodded.

"Not all of them, of course. Some I like rather more than others."

"Naturally enough."

In his final year, he fell in with a group from his college who had a reputation for riotous living. He had heard of their parties, but had never been invited. Now, unexpectedly, a card was put under his door, inviting him for drinks.

The other guests were formally dressed, and he felt embarrassed at his ordinary suit and brown shoes, but his host engaged him in earnest conversation, and drinks were poured. Everybody present was polished, elegant; there were signs of the generous allowance, too; an ornate decanter with a silver top; heavy crystal glasses; a silver cigarette box, engraved.

"Tell me, what's it like in Africa?"

"It?"

"The whole deal, the whole place. Do you live in one of those white Highland type places, you know, bungalows, servants and the rest?"

"I suppose so."

"Somebody to polish your shoes?"

"Yes."

"And you go in to breakfast in the morning and it's all laid out under silver trays? Kedgeree, eggs, all the trimmings?"

"Some people live like that. Most people don't."

Another joined in.

"It's all pretty unjust though, isn't it? Servants aren't paid very much, are they?"

"No. They aren't. And it is unjust."

There was disappointment.

"I thought you might try and justify it. Surely there's something you can say in its favour. The White Man's Burden?"

Their host interjected. "Excuse them, Michael. They don't realise it's terribly rude to tell people that they come from an unjust society. Heavens! Who doesn't, I ask you? Look at us!"

He was invited back two weeks later, and again after that. There were different people present on each occasion, but all of the same sort. The faces changed, and the names, but the conversation followed much the same lines. He realised that he was favoured in some way, and that he was the only one who was always asked back.

His host said to him: "You amuse me so much, Michael. You're unlike the rest of these perfectly poisonous people who populate this place. You're so . . . so straight. And I mean that in the best of senses. You're straightforward. You're not a snob, or a poseur, or anything like that. You're just pure goodness, do you realise that? Pure goodness!"

They were alone, with a half-finished bottle of hock on the table.

"Would there be room for somebody like me in a place like Bulawayo? What could I do there? Don't answer! Don't answer! Just drink up!"

He reached across and filled his guest's glass.

"I've drunk enough already. This is our second bottle."

"But it's good for you, this German stuff! It's terribly mild, you know. They make it like that so that you can drink two, three bottles without ill effects."

He emptied his glass, and leaned against the back of the sofa.

Then: "Don't go home tonight. Stay here."

He looked at his host, who was on his feet, bottle in hand. The other held his stare, and smiled. He could not mean what he thought he meant.

He shook his head. "No. I must get going."

"Why? Stay. What does it matter? Look, what does it matter what you've had drummed into you. It doesn't matter in the slightest. It's not an important thing. Stay."

He stood up, slightly unsteady on his feet.

"I don't want to," he said. "I just don't want to stay."

He walked towards the door. His host had now put down the bottle and had taken a cigarette from the silver cigarette box.

"Southern Rhodesia," he laughed. "Southern Rhodesia!"

He stopped. "I don't know what you mean."

"Quite. You haven't kicked over the traces of that backwater, that's what I mean."

He said nothing. He stared at the face of the other, bemused.

"Do you want to know something, Michael? Rhodes was queer, didn't you know. Rhodes himself! Funny, isn't it? They should have put that on his monument. I can just see it, can't you?"

The invitations stopped. He still saw the others, of course, and his would-be seducer too; Cambridge was too small a place to allow avoidance. There were smiles, waves — as if nothing had happened, but for Michael the single encounter had changed everything.

Nothing was as it seemed any more; the dons, the undergraduates, the whole edifice of a civilised, clever society concealed within it a petty heart. It was hypocrisy. These people were no different from the small town drinkers and adulterers of Bulawayo.

"You've dropped your new friends. What went wrong? Couldn't pour enough wine down your throat?"

"They've dropped me. Not that I care."

There was a silence. "Good."

"You didn't like them?"

"Who does? Anyway, what do you think they saw in you?"

He looked at his friend. Had he known all along; had it been that obvious to others?

"I don't know. Perhaps they misjudged me."

His friend laughed.

"That's one way of putting it. They were barking up the wrong tree. It's really rather funny. I can just hear them. 'He's not one of the players after all! My dear, can you believe it!' "

Without the social distraction, he redoubled his efforts with his work. His tutors were encouraging, and hints were dropped that he might like to stay on for research. There were applied mathematics projects which needed people; he could find something in one of these, they were sure of it.

He was tempted. It would have been

simple to accept the offer and spend the next three years safely ensconced in a well-funded project in Cambridge. He almost accepted, but one afternoon, in a small village outside Cambridge, where he had been invited to lunch with friends at a pub, he saw a sky which reminded him of Africa. For a moment he was still, and then he caught that unique, evocative smell — the smell of rain on dust. For a moment, some fluke of air and water brought Africa to that flat, quiet part of England, and his heart lurched.

The offer of the research grant was turned down, which astonished his tutors.

"You really can't expect anything like this to come up again," one said to him. "If you're serious about mathematics, then this is the point at which you must decide."

"I've already decided."

"You're making a mistake. There's nothing for you there. There can't be!"

He bit his lip. How could this man, with his rarefied, academic manner, know anything about Africa? He wanted to say that; to tell him that the tug of the heart could not be denied, but he did not, and mumbled something about having obligations to the place. The tutor, silenced, turned his attention to something else, and Michael knew that this was the writing-off. He had been offered his pass to a world which the tutor, and those like him, saw as being the best possible world to which anybody might aspire, and he had ungratefully turned it down.

A few weeks later, he received a letter from the headmaster of a boys' private school outside Bulawayo. He had heard that he was about to graduate, and wondered if he could possibly induce him to accept a post. It was a shame that so many of the country's promising young men never came back; would he prove this not to be true?

He wrote back, accepting the offer. He posted the letter in a letterbox outside the college porter's box, and as he slipped it into the box, he felt a further distance opening up between himself and Cambridge. There was nothing more for him here; it had been interesting, but no more. This cold, small country meant nothing to him.

He was relaxed. "It's been a marvellous day, Michael. Well done."

"Thankyou." He took her father's outstretched hand. "I mean it. Thankyou."

"You're family now. You don't have to thank me."

He inclined his head slightly, acknowledging the embarrassing compliment. "But I'm still grateful. And I know that Anne . . ."

The other smiled. "You should give your children a good send-off. Anyway, I know that she's in safe hands with you."

"Of course."

He glanced surreptitiously at his watch. The train was due to leave in half an hour and they would have to find the number of their coach, pay the porters and sort everything else out.

"Yes. It's time." He turned away and signalled to one of the waiters. "I'll tell him to let the driver know. It won't take you longer than ten minutes."

Outside, on the steps of the City Hall, the guests had lined up for the their departure. Many of them had cartons of confetti and some of the children were already tossing it about. He looked out and winced.

"Are you ready?"

Anne was at his side, dressed in the dress that he had helped her choose at Meikles, wearing the hat that her mother had bought her in Salisbury. She held on to his arm, pinching the flesh playfully.

"Come on." She turned to her mother, who was hovering at her side. He had never seen them show any sign of physical affection, but now she was in her mother's arms. They embraced, the mother patting her back, whispering something to her.

Her father smiled and winked at him conspiratorially: "A woman never leaves her mother, I'm told. Look at that."

Then she turned to embrace her father. He noticed the tears in her eyes and the flush on her cheeks. Her father held her gently, pushing her away after a few moments.

"You'll be late," he said. "Remember that we'll be seeing you in a week or so anyway."

She was sobbing. "You'll be all right? Will you be all right?"

They all laughed. "Of course, darling. You silly girl. We've been all right for years. Years."

Then, in the car, she leaned against him and they kissed. She smelled of a perfume which was new to him — something expensive, exotic. He swept her hair back from her eyes and loosened his tie. She touched him playfully on his chest.

"A week," she said. "A week, with nobody else, and nothing to do but look at the Falls."

"Tremendous," he said.

The car moved off. Some of the guests were still standing in clusters about the gates of the car park; they waved. Two young men reached out and thumped the top of the car; he smiled and waved to them.

People looked at the car. A cyclist moved over to the side of the road, a black man in torn shabby khaki and wearing a dilapidated cap. He looked into the car, his face expressionless, and then looked away again, as if dazzled by her dress.

Within a few minutes they were at the station. The driver stopped, got out of the car, and whistled for a porter to take the suitcases.

Then they made their way on to the platform and inspected the list of sleeping car accommodation. It was strange for him to see their names together; she pointed it out, and touched his arm.

"That's us. Husband and wife, you see!"

As the train pulled out of the town he struggled with the thick leather strap of a corridor window. Eventually the heavy glass window slid down and he was able to lean out into the night air. It was fresh, and he felt its sobering effect. It was almost dark now, and as the train swayed slowly on its way they could see the lights of the African township burning in neat rows, out towards the edge of the bush and the flat plains of Matabeleland. The line swung slowly away from the city and he was able to see the fire of the engine as they negotiated a bend in the track. Sparks flew up from the boiler, flitting like fireflies into the thick darkness of the night. Other windows were open further up the train and he saw the dark shapes of the occupants. He would leave the window open for the fresh air, even if it meant that smuts of coal dust would come in from the steam engine ahead. He knocked before he entered the compartment. She was standing up as he went in, folding her going-away dress into a suitcase.

"Can I help you with anything?"

She shook her head. "Everything's fine. I've

put your pyjamas out on your bunk. And your toothbrush is over there."

The words sounded so strange to him. Was this what marriage would be about; talking about little arrangements — your meal's ready, don't forget your keys, have you seen my pen, and so on? Would they talk like that? And if they didn't, what else was there to talk about?

He sat down on the bunk. Did she think that he had slept with anyone before? She would not have done so — he was certain of that — and they had never gone far themselves. She was a virgin, he knew that. He looked at her: she was now his wife. The men had alluded to it so much at university, although he had disliked the smuttiness and crudity. Would this be what all the embarrassment, the physical itchiness, the talk, would be about? What would it be? The sweatiness of skin against skin? Fumbling about in a bunk bed narrow for one, impossible for two?

She smiled at him. She was embarrassed too; he could see that. He would have to do something to help her. He looked about him; the light — he could turn that off. Then they could get undressed in the dark and each save the blushes of the other.

He rose to his feet and she gave a start.

"Don't worry," he said. "I'm not going to hurt you."

71

She laughed. "I didn't think . . ."

He switched out the light, but instead of total darkness there was a glow from a night light above the door. There would be a switch for that too, but where?

They ate breakfast in the swaying restaurant car, watching the land roll past. The trees were higher now and the bush much thicker; this was no longer cattle country, but untamed land, elephant territory. He sat back in his seat and watched the early morning sun on the forest's canopy of trees. He knew what the bush was like here. During his three months' spell of military training he had been on patrol in country just like this. He had spent ten days in a camp cut off from the outside world, shooting for the pot, feeling dirtier as each day passed, prowling through the six-feet-high grass in an elaborate game of overgrown boy scouts. And soon, on the horizon, above the sea of tree tops, they saw the cloud of spray. He offered her his seat, which had a better view, but the tracks suddenly began to turn and the forest closed in again.

"Half an hour," he said. "Half an hour at the most."

She went back to the compartment to pack, leaving him at the table. He poured himself another cup of coffee and stared at the tablecloth. He felt trapped, a feeling not unlike the feeling he had experienced when he had first been sent off to boarding school. He had been driven there by his father and had been aware of the complete impossibility of escape. This was how he now felt: a prison of walls and barbed wire could not have been more constricting.

"Don't expect to enjoy your honeymoon," a cynical colleague had said to him. "Nobody ever does."

To his relief, the feeling passed. That evening, as they sat on the terrace of the hotel and watched the last of the sun in the cloud of spray, he felt relaxed again. They had been joined for sundowners by another young couple whose room was in the same corridor as their own. He was an engineer with the Goldfields company; she worked for an accountant in Bulawayo. Their presence seemed to act as a catalyst for Michael, and she noticed this. He's better with other people about him, she thought; he's gregarious. That didn't matter, of course, she liked company herself and would be quite happy to be sociable. Honeymoons, she had thought, are meant to be times for privacy, but there would be time enough for that in the future. There were years ahead with just the two of them, although that afternoon she had found morbid thoughts coming upon her, unwelcomed. She had imagined him dying in some way, here at the Falls, perhaps slipping on a rock in the rain forest on the lip of one of the gorges and falling hundreds of feet into the river below. She had read of that happening to another honeymoon couple and she could imagine the desolation. She pictured herself returning, a widow, to the sympathy of her parents, bearing the name of a dead husband and memories of a married life measured in hours. She struggled to dispel these thoughts, just as, when she was ten years old, she had dispelled fears of the death of her parents.

They sat outside until the first mosquitoes began to trouble them. Then they went inside and bathed before dinner. Although they had made no arrangement to meet again that night, the other couple beckoned them over to their table and they joined them. She felt a momentary surge of anger at the intrusion, but suppressed it and joined in the mood of the evening. Wine was ordered; she felt it go quickly to her head, making her feel light, almost dizzy. The other woman became flushed and laughed in a shrieking way whenever her husband made some witticism. Michael drank lager with his food, keeping pace with the other man.

By ten o'clock they were the last people in the dining room, watched over by several patient waiters too cowed to protest at the extension of their normal hours. When they rose to leave, the waiters swooped on the tablecloth and the empty glasses. They returned to their room, saying goodnight to their friends in the corridor. Then, the door closed behind them, she kicked off her shoes and flung herself on the bed. He stood at the door for a moment, as if uncertain.

"My God, I'm tired," he said. "I could sleep for hours."

She looked at him. "Why not? You're on holiday."

He crossed to the other side of the room. "I mean, I'm really tired," he said. And then, as if suddenly seized of an idea: "Why don't I sleep on cushions tonight? On the floor? We'd both get the sleep we need."

She did nothing. He thought for a moment that her eyes were closed and that she had gone to sleep, but then he noticed that she was watching him. He tossed his head back and laughed.

"Don't take me seriously," he said. "I'm only joking."

She giggled. "I didn't," she said. "Of course I didn't take you seriously."

The school lay thirty miles outside Bulawayo. It had been built in the thirties, at a time when there was a demand for private education from those who would otherwise have been inclined to send their sons out of the country, to expensive boys' schools in the Transvaal or Natal. It was modelled unselfconsciously on the pattern of the English public school, and liked to employ Oxbridge men. After the War, the supply of such graduates declined just as the fortunes of the tobacco planters and ranchers improved. The expansion of the school meant that graduates of South African universities were considered, second-generation Southern Rhodesians; gentlemen, nonetheless, as the headmaster insisted.

The site for the school had been well chosen. It was built on land donated to the first board of governors by a wealthy cattle rancher who saw the gesture as a possible way of securing an education for an ineducable son. There was more land than the school could possibly use, several hundred acres in fact, cleared out of the low scrub bush on the side of a range of hills. It was a healthy spot, dry, and cooler than the hot plains over which it looked. Gum trees had been planted as the buildings were constructed and these now provided welcome shade in the height of the hot season. There were playing fields, irrigated from the sluggish green river that flowed a mile away from the main buildings, and a small farm which the members of the school farming club ran.

The nearest settlement was ten miles away, at a point where a few stores clustered around a junction on the strip-road that led south to the Limpopo and the South African border. There was a mission school there, staffed by two German priests and several African teachers, and, some distance further along, a small gold mine, the last of the mines to operate in the area. In the bush around the school itself, there remained the old workings of the earlier mines, dangerous, unprotected shafts and tunnels that bored into the hard red-white earth.

On his marriage, Michael was moved out of the single staff quarters, a long, low, rather barrack-like building near the rugby fields, into one of the junior staff houses. It was a bungalow, one of the earliest buildings raised on the site, and was considered by the other staff to be the bottom of the housing ladder. The roof, which was made of corrugated iron, protested loudly against its restraining bolts as the morning sun heated it up; the bath, an ancient tub on claw feet brought from a demolished house in Bulawayo, was chronically uncomfortable, and the kitchen was regularly invaded by ants. Anne, however, chose to defend it on the grounds of its character and surprised everybody by saying that she wanted to remain there rather than move when a better house became available.

Michael seemed largely indifferent to it. He cursed the ants, laying down ineffective poisons for them, and he hated the way the verandah let in the sun at the wrong times, but for him a house was a place to eat and sleep in, not a thing to exercise the imagination or the emotions. He converted the spare bedroom into a study and would sit there when he had to write a letter or fill in report forms on the boys; for the rest, though, he always seemed to be at the school or visiting other staff members in their house.

Anne did her best to create a home. She studied pattern books and made curtains for the windows; she replaced some of the furniture with items given her by her parents, and she hung paintings which she bought in a small art shop in Bulawayo. They were reproductions of Constable and Turner, symbols of the culture to which they all knew they belonged, which was the reason for their presence there in Africa, but which seemed so distant, so impossibly beautiful in the midst of the pervasive dust and beneath the hot dome of the sky.

Michael scarcely looked at the pictures; he felt unmoved by them. His ideal of beauty, if he had ever bothered to define it, would be a Cape valley with towering blue mountains behind it and a Cape Dutch farmhouse on the lower slopes.

They settled awkwardly into their married life. Anne was busy with the house and filled her days that way, although she knew that the time would come when the curtains were all made and the sitting room completely decorated, and what then? The African cook did all the cooking and the cleaning of the kitchen; it would have been unthinkable for her to take on responsibility for that. So what would there be for her to do?

She looked at the lives led by the other wives. They fell into two groups, the older ones, who spent their mornings drinking coffee together and playing bridge, and the younger ones, who had children. She was tried out by the bridge players, but she lacked interest in the game and found it difficult to concentrate on remembering which cards went out. She withdrew from bridge and dallied with the young mothers; but they had concerns which seemed petty to her and from their point of view they were merely waiting for her to become pregnant and to share their interests.

Sundays were the worst of days. During the week, Michael would immerse himself in his duties at the school and could find a reason for absence from the house; on most Saturdays, his responsibilities for the boys' sports would keep him busy all day, often, for away games, in Bulawayo itself. On Sundays, however, there was no sport, and it was a school custom that the boys would be left to their own devices around the hostels or encouraged to go out on day-long expeditions into the surrounding country. She would sit in the house with Michael, reading or listening to records, but he would begin to feel restless and would go out for a walk. She offered to accompany him, and did so on one or two occasions, but it became clear to her that he wanted to be by himself. He would walk out ahead, and then wait for her to catch up, an expression of irritation on his face. She stopped going with him, and would wait on the verandah, paging through a magazine or working on the *Bulawayo Chronicle* crossword puzzle, but all the time willing him back. She needed his presence, even if he seemed to be indifferent to her company. She liked just to sit and look at him, savouring his undoubted handsomeness. She thought of him as a beautiful animal — a young tawny lion, or a leopard perhaps — who had wandered into her life and had to be guarded. She thought his distant behaviour might be nothing more than his maleness, his otherness. She had no right to expect him to settle down like a domestic cat.

Her parents waited for an invitation before they made the journey to visit them. She had seen them briefly on their return to Bulawayo after the honeymoon, but she had hesitated to ask them to the house until a few weeks later. This was her separate life now, her adult life, and they would come into it as invited guests rather than as parents.

She had arranged for them to come for dinner one Saturday and then to stay overnight before returning to the farm the following morning. They arrived with a car full of presents; bits and pieces for the house, sticks of biltong from kudu he had shot on the farm, books from her childhood: her inscribed Bible, her swimming prize, her ballet album. She laughed at these mementoes of childhood but was secretly pleased.

The four of them sat on the verandah for sundowners. The conversation was largely about the house and the school. Anne's father sought details of the fate of schemes which he had been involved in as a governor: the new pavilions, the expansion of the fields, the new house for the headmaster. Then, over dinner, the conversation seemed to dwell on family friends of theirs, whom Michael did not know. He listened to the chatter and then, pleading tiredness, went to bed.

"So, you're happy then, as a married woman?" her father asked. "Your new life going well?"

She avoided his eyes. "Of course. It's all so different. This house, this place, everything . . ."

"But you're happy?" he persisted.

Her mother intervened. "Of course she is. It's different for her. It's all new."

"I'm sorry," her father said, smiling. "I was just checking up that all was going well. I've always wanted to know that my girl's all right. There's nothing wrong with that."

He met his wife's hostile gaze and then looked away.

"I'm sorry, darling. I don't want to pry. We're a tiny family, now . . . You're very precious . . ." He stopped. There was a silence in the room. He had his hands folded on his lap, his wife was looking up at the ceiling. Anne, sitting next to him, leaned across and put her arm around his shoulder.

"I'll tell you if there's anything wrong," she said. "Don't worry. I promise I'll tell you."

Several weeks after this visit, he had to accompany a school team into Bulawayo for a rugby match. She had not gone with him on one of such trips before, but she could not face the prospect of a Saturday by herself and asked him to take her. They drove into town in silence; she assumed that his mind was on the forthcoming game, which he had announced they were bound to lose, and so she did not attempt to engage him in conversation. When they reached the host school, he swung the car into a parking place under a jacaranda tree and turned to her.

"I'm sure you'll be bored," he said dryly. "It's only rugby, you know."

She felt the resentment in his comment. He feels I'm intruding, she thought. I shouldn't have come.

"I know," she replied airily. "But even rugby has its moments."

He shrugged his shoulders, opening his door to get out.

"Only if you know the rules." A pause. "I take it you don't?"

She smiled. "Some of them. Offsides. High tackles. Things like that."

He moved away from the car. "You can sit over there if you like. There'll be an audience of sorts."

She looked towards the small, rickety stand that stood under the line of trees beside the field. She had imagined watching the game with him, seated by him — which was the entire reason for her coming — where was he going to be? Why did he have to go away? The coach carrying the boys had now arrived and his team had spilled out to walk towards the changing rooms. Michael went with them, the centre of a circle of admiring boys. She heard him laugh at something that one of the boys had said and she saw him pat one on the shoulder in a gesture of encouragement; exclusion.

Throughout the game he sat crouched down on the touchlines, shouting out to his team, urging them on. He looked at her once briefly during the half-time break, and he gave a half-hearted wave, but that was the only recognition. She tried to concentrate on the game, even if only to be able to say something to him about it afterwards, but it was unintelligible to her. She concluded that his team was losing, as most of the time the ball seemed to be in the possession of the other side, but she had no idea of the score.

At the end, she climbed down from the stand and strolled across to where he was standing with a small group of masters from his school and the other. As he saw her coming he frowned and separated himself from his companions.

"Well?" he asked, his expression neutral. "How did you enjoy it?"

"I'm sorry we lost. The boys did their best."

He snorted. "We didn't lose. We won."

She grimaced. "I thought I was beginning to understand it. Are you sure we won?"

"Of course." He looked down at his watch and glanced over his shoulder at the other men.

"Are we going straight back?" she asked. "I wondered if we should stay for dinner in Bulawayo. Perhaps we could do a film at the Princes. We could see what's on."

He looked down at the ground. "Well . . . well, I was rather thinking of talking about the match with the chaps back there . . ." He gestured in the direction of his companions. "Just a short while at the pub. Perhaps you could . . . you could go and see the Marshalls or somebody like that. They'd be at home. They always are."

She caught her breath. Then: "Would you be long?"

His expression brightened. "No. An hour

maybe. Something like that."

She felt the anger well up inside her, and her throat was tight as she answered.

"How would I know when to collect you?"

He thought for a while. "I've got an idea. Why don't you run yourself back home whenever you like? That would be simplest, wouldn't it? I'll come back with Jack or one of the others."

He looked at her hopefully. She hesitated for a few moments, during which she saw him prepare to be belligerent. It was not worth it, even if she could stand up to him.

"I see. Well, if that's what you want."

He was like a schoolboy given permission to take the afternoon off. He leaned forward, held her lightly by the shoulders, and kissed her. She felt the tight line of his lips against her cheek; passionless; the faint odour of shaving cream from his skin; the soft pressure of his hands through the fabric of her dress. And behind him, the line of tree tops swaying in the warm breeze and the boys in their bright colours.

She returned to the car. She fumbled with the key in the lock as she opened the door; her hands were shaking and her breathing was irregular, but she fought back the tears that she knew would flow once she gave in to them. He had turned away now, anyway, and would not see her, but there were others around. She saw the boys tossing a rugby ball to one another, and she realised that she hated them. They were crude, aggressive, unfinished; they exuded a quality which she found physically distasteful. She could not imagine how anyone could find a teenage boy desirable, and she knew that there were women who did, but in her eyes they were raw, threatening creatures, untamed.

By the time she arrived at the farm, it had been dark for an hour. She saw the lights of the farmhouse as she came over the hill above the vlei and she pressed her foot down on the accelerator, sending the car bumping wildly over the rain corrugations that had appeared in the road's eroded surface. As she drew up in front of the house, her father appeared at the front door, a large flashlight in his hand. He swung the beam towards the open door of her car and then walked over to meet her.

"There's nothing wrong, is there?"

She got out of the car and swept back the hair from her forehead. She felt the fine white dust from the road on her skin, a prickly feeling that made her long for a bath.

"No."

He flashed the beam of the torch into the car to see if there was anybody with her. He said nothing, but the question hung in the air between them.

"Michael's in Bulawayo with a team," she explained. "He was a bit tied up. I thought

I'd just come out and see you. I'll stay overnight and drive back tomorrow."

Her father relaxed. "I see. Well, we're always happy for you to be here — you know that. Stay as long as you can."

She understood that the invitation meant more than it said; that he was telling her that if she wanted to leave her husband, then they would welcome her back. For a moment she felt resentment at the implication that her marriage had failed. Then she saw her mother appear in the doorway and, very briefly, she pictured them alone in the rambling house, with nothing to do in the evenings but think of their dead son and the daughter they saw once a month.

She said nothing more about the reason for her presence. She doubted if her parents accepted her explanation, but that did not matter; whatever their doubts, they would have to remain unexpressed. This suited the relationship she had with them, a relationship which had never progressed to one of adult equality. She had hidden things from them as a child, and continued to do so now. Both sides knew this, and both yearned to be able to speak to the other, but accepted the seeming impossibility of intimacy.

They had already had dinner, but sat with her as she ate her meal in the dining room. They talked about her house, about the improvements she had made, about family friends — of whom there was no fresh news, since nothing really ever happened — and about developments on the farm. It was a conversation they had had before, and which they would have again over breakfast. She knew that her father would have liked to talk politics, to discuss the latest speech by Welensky or to wonder what Whitehead would do, but she took only a slight interest in these matters and could not say much that would interest him.

After dinner, there was nothing to do but to have a bath and go to bed. She lay for almost half an hour in the warmth of the discoloured water from the rainwater tanks, wondering about what he would think when he returned home to find the house empty. It had occurred to her that he might think that she had been involved in an accident and that she should perhaps telephone somebody to put a note on the door, but she decided against this. It was a matter of pride now; let him wonder, let him be punished.

She returned the following afternoon, anxious about what he would say to her, but prepared to defend herself. She disliked confrontation, preferring to compromise or back down, but on this occasion she was prepared to fight. She had mentally rehearsed what she would say to him; if he made accusations, well, she could respond.

She parked the car by the side of the

house and went in by the back door. There was no sign of him in the sitting room, nor in the bedroom. The bed had been slept in and his wardrobe was open, but otherwise there was no clue as to his whereabouts. As it was a Sunday there would be nothing for him to do in the school. She made herself some tea and drank it on the verandah. She now began to feel concerned; had he left her?

She finished the tea, deciding to go and ask the couple in the neighbouring house if they had seen him. Her welcome was abnormal. There was something unusual in her neighbour's attitude, an element of surprise, perhaps, or even caginess.

"He's gone for a walk," she was told. "Or I think he went for a walk."

She felt relieved. "I see."

She felt that she had to offer some explanation. "I was away last night. I stayed in Bulawayo, or rather, I went to my parents' farm."

Her neighbour hesitated. "You weren't with Michael?"

"No. As I told you, I was at the farm." She now knew that something had happened. She regretted her anger and was now only concerned for him. An accident?

"Something happened?"

The neighbour looked embarrassed. "Yes," she said. "I gather that he went off with Jim and Paul and . . ."

"They got drunk?" There was nothing un-toward in that. Everybody drank, often too much.

The neighbour continued: "He did more than that. He brought a crate of beer back and went and gave it to the boys."

Anne laughed. "Is that all?" Her neighbour looked at her in surprise.

"All?"

"Yes. It's not as if . . . as if he assaulted somebody or something like that."

The other woman shrugged. "You might think it nothing. The Head's furious. The boys drank the beer. The Head heard them shouting their heads off. They let off two fire extinguishers before they were stopped."

She heard him going into his study. He must know that I'm home, she thought; he will have seen the car. For a few minutes she stayed where she was in the sitting room and then, on impulse, she got up and went to his room. He was sitting at his desk, toying with a pencil. He did not look at her as she walked across the room to reach his side and put her arm around him.

"So. Here we are."

He did not reply. He had a pencil in his hands which he continued to study.

"I'm sorry, Michael. I really am."

He fiddled with the pencil, then, quietly: "Where were you?"

"At the farm. I went there because you seemed not to want me around." She paused. "I'm sorry that I went. I didn't mean to let you down."

He did not sound annoyed.

"I'm in trouble here," he said, after a while. "There's going to be one hell of a row."

"I heard from Joan. She told me." She paused. "It seems a storm in a teacup, if you ask me."

"He'll probably ask me to leave. You know what he's like."

She had wondered whether that would happen, but had concluded that even a man as pompous as he was would be bound to give somebody a chance. What did it matter if a few boys drank a few bottles of beer? They did so all the time when they were at home — the sneaked bottle from the pantry, the half glass with their father. The whole country relied on cold beer in the hot months.

She said nothing more and they stood there for a few awkward minutes, her arm still resting on his shoulder. Then, almost imperceptibly at first, she felt him move away from under her.

That evening he called at the Headmaster's house, aware of the eyes watching him and gloating — he suspected — at the sight of his discomfort. I'm like a schoolboy going to be disciplined, he thought.

The atmosphere, though, was cordial.

"I'm very sorry about what happened last night."

The Headmaster took off his glasses and gave them an unnecessary polish. "So am I. It's, well, I'm afraid it can only be called disgraceful."

"I know. I had too much to drink in Bulawayo."

"So I understand. It's not so much that, of course. It's the question of how the boys can possibly respect you after what's happened."

He realised that this revealed the decision — dismissal. "It's difficult to continue in post after one's been compromised," the Headmaster went on. "The boys sense vulnerability . . ."

Like you, he thought. And then, in sudden alarm, he realised what dismissal would mean. There would be no job for him in Bulawayo, probably not even in Salisbury; the country was too small to allow people to start again. He would have to plead in mitigation; he would need this man's pity.

"I'm very sorry. Things, you see, have just been very hard for me."

The Headmaster raised an eyebrow. "Hard for you? Frankly, that rather surprises me. You've had everything going for you — good job, prospects, charming wife." There was a look of disdain on his face; self-pity had been sensed and it repelled.

"My marriage. Things have been a bit rocky."

The Headmaster hesitated. "Your marriage hasn't been going well?"

"No, it hasn't," he said.

"We all have our ups and downs," the Headmaster said. "You should expect that. You have to take them in your stride." He gestured vaguely out of the window. "I could tell you about matrimonial difficulties of one sort or another in virtually all of those houses. Fact of life."

It was not working. He thought for a moment, and then: "It's worse than that. I . . . . You see, I can't make love to my wife. It's unconsummated."

For a moment there was no change in the older man's expression, but after a few seconds he lost his composure. He seemed deflated, as if his entire position had suddenly been cut from beneath his feet.

"My dear chap . . . Look, I'm terribly sorry to hear that. You see . . . You . . ." He tailed off.

It's outside his experience, Michael thought. The initiative was entirely his.

"It's not physical, if you know what I mean. It's just that there's something inside me, something mental. It's a psychological problem I suppose."

"I see." He became silent, looking away from Michael. Moving to the window, he traced a pattern in the dust on the ledge, and then turned again. "I suppose that puts a different complexion on matters. You must be . . . you must be under very considerable strain. Something like that . . ."

"Yes. I am."

He drew in his breath and looked directly at Michael, still struggling with embarrassment but now remembering the whole point of the interview.

"I'm prepared to overlook last night," he said. "Provided you make some attempt to sort out your difficulties. What about a doctor? Have you spoken to anyone?"

"No." Adding mentally: not even to my wife.

"Well, it so happens that I know somebody in Bulawayo." He was in control again, managing, coping, as a headmaster faced with a crisis must be seen to do. "An expert in these . . . nervous problems. I'll give him a ring. He'll see you, I'm sure. Dr Leberman. Charming chap. Jewish. Very astute."

He said nothing to Anne about the interview other than to tell her that his apology had been accepted and that the incident was over. He did not mention the doctor; his failure as a husband had never been alluded to or even acknowledged — she had started to talk to him when they returned from the Falls — merely to say that if there was anything she

94

was doing which was wrong, or unhelpful . . . but he had left the room. Since then, she had taken her cue from him and it had been like a cancer denied: nothing said, but the malignancy ever-present, growing.

He regretted almost immediately his confession to the Headmaster. As he went over in his mind the painful minutes in his employer's study, he was struck by the absurdity of the outcome. If he had been serious in the suggestion that he see the doctor in Bulawayo, then what it amounted to was a conditional sentence. He felt as if he had been convicted of an offence but allowed to go free in return for submitting to treatment. He had read of this being done in the courts to people such as voyeurs or exhibitionists — the sad, pathetic offence condoned in exchange for the aversive electric shocks or the libido-suppressing drugs. And he had agreed.

He had made up his mind not to go, but a note had arrived with a telephone number and an address and, almost out of curiosity alone, he had phoned for an appointment. The receptionist, who spoke with the clipped, singsong accent of Johannesburg, told him that he could be seen the following week.

He became increasingly nervous as the day of the appointment approached. On that morning, he was awake by five, and he rushed through to the bathroom, where he was sick. He bent over the pan, his knees on the cold stone slabs of the floor, the odour of strong disinfectant in his nostrils. I don't have to do it; I don't have to tell anyone. I can lie. I can carry on lying.

But he made the journey nonetheless, and parked his car in Borrow Street, where the doctors had their consulting rooms. He hesitated at the door of the surgery. It would be easy to stop at this point, to walk out of the building and into the bar of the Selbourne Hotel, but he decided to ring the bell — there was nothing to be lost in at least seeing this Dr Leberman.

Inside, he was shown into a small waiting room where he sat for ten minutes until a door opened and Dr Leberman called him into his room. The doctor was a slightly fleshy man, grey-haired, wearing a pair of old-fashioned unrimmed glasses. He ushered Michael in and gestured to a chair at the side of his table. There's no couch, Michael thought.

The doctor smiled at him as he sat down and began the consultation with questions about the school and Michael's work. His questions were put casually and were disarming in their effect. Michael answered them conversationally, barely noticing the direction they were taking, which was towards his own experiences there and his own feelings. By the time they had reached the end of their hour-long session, he felt comfortable in the doctor's company and was talking quite frankly. Nothing was said about the reason for the consultation, though; in his mind it had been little more than a social conversation, and a particularly pleasant one at that.

They met the following week, and the week after that. At the second session, they touched on Michael's problem, although it was still indirectly talked about. He noticed that the doctor picked up and used his own euphemisms and did not refer directly to what had really brought him to the therapist's chair. There was talk of his "anxieties" and his "matrimonial difficulties" — never anything more specific.

At the third meeting, though, it seemed to Michael as if something had changed between them. Dr Leberman appeared to be less interested in the generalities with which they had previously concerned themselves and started to ask questions which were more direct, more probing. He wanted to know how Michael felt about Anne — did he find her attractive? Did he look forward to her company when he was away from her? What did he expect of her in the marriage? Of course he had no answers to these questions, or, at least, no answers which appeared to satisfy Dr Leberman. Yes, he found her attractive, but even as he said that he realised that his reply lacked conviction.

Dr Leberman noticed the hesitation and

sat quietly, waiting for further elucidation.

"She's a very attractive woman. People have often said that. I'm lucky." He hesitated; more seemed to be required. "She's got a very good figure too. She's in good shape."

"You find her sexually attractive too?"

"Of course." He was silent again. The doctor's eyes, understanding, piercing, were fixed on him. They could tell, Michael knew, that he was lying.

"And yet you can't make love to her?"

"No." It was the second admission, but this time, unlike the occasion in the Headmaster's study, it was not made in desperation. This was a completely flat acknowledgement, as a man admitting a failure.

"And do you think that you could make love to any woman, to others?"

Michael stood up. For a moment Dr Leberman looked concerned, thinking that his patient was going to storm out of the room, but it was only to move to the window. He stood there, looking down on the street below. They were five floors up, near the top of the building, and below them the wide sweep of the street ran die-straight to the brown edge of the city. His voice was almost inaudible, but loud enough for the doctor to hear.

"No. Not really."

He told her that he was spending these afternoons in the library in town, that he was preparing new courses for the following year. She did not believe him; there was no sign of any notes or any explanation of what the new courses were. She knew that his interests were firmly unintellectual, that he was happiest as a physical education teacher and that he treated any other duties as a chore. She immediately assumed that what took him into Bulawayo was an affair, and that the passion he denied her was directed elsewhere. She imagined his afternoons in a hotel in the town, with some bored woman from one of the wealthy suburbs, perhaps a married woman, delighting in her handsome plaything.

The sessions with Dr Leberman made no difference to his relationship with his wife. They were polite to one another, although he was clearly bored. They talked, but only at a superficial level, and their bed was as arid as ever. He offered no explanation and volunteered no tenderness; injured, she withdrew into a private world, avoiding the company of other women, spending her days in reading or listening to the radio, beginning, but rarely finishing, letters to school friends with whom she had long since lost touch.

She began to feel that the cause of her unhappiness was herself, that she was to blame for his coolness. She studied her face in the bedroom mirror and scrutinised her unclothed body in the bathroom. What was wrong with her? Why could she not arouse him? She decided that she was plain and she raided the cosmetic counter of a large department store in town; she spent money on clothes; she did exercises on the bathroom floor in order to keep her weight down. But the odds seemed stacked against her. Her cheekbones were too low; her eyes were the wrong shape; her breasts were too small; the weather dried her skin.

Slowly, as the notion of his developing affair grew in her mind, she started to think that her only hope of tearing him away from his lover in Bulawayo would be to make him jealous. She could find a lover herself. She could have an affair. She would let him guess at it, let him wonder, and then not bother to hide it. He would hate it; all men did. For Anne the thought of a lover had a further attraction. She was stung by the thought that she, a married woman, was still a virgin. If her inexperience were to blame for the asexuality of their marriage, then she could remedy that. She would gain experience which she would then use to lure him back to her.

She had talked to nobody. It was a matter of pride first and foremost, even although she knew that it was not her fault. But others would think differently. If a husband did not make love to his wife that was usually because he didn't find her attractive. It was the wife's fault. She inhibited him; put him off; she was doing something that she shouldn't be doing; whatever it was, it was the wife's fault. That's what people thought, and that's what they would think in her case. And even if he was having an affair — which he probably was — they would think that he was seeing another woman because of something she had done. The marriage was too new for it to be anything but that.

So she kept it to herself until she could no longer bear the burden. She had to speak about it, to confess it, to have reassurance that this was his problem, not hers. She turned to an old friend. She had gone through school with her and although she had seen little of her since the wedding, the friendship had always been close and relaxed. They had talked about boyfriends before; there was nothing they could not share.

They met for lunch. Her friend, Susan, had chosen the restaurant from the tiny choice available — the top floor of the Hotel Victoria, a featureless brown building which was the best that the city could offer. They sat at a table near a window which gave them a view of the town and the plains beyond. Susan gushed, as she always did when they met up, and shot questions at her. How was the house? Had she bought the curtains yet? Had she taken any furniture from the farm? Was Michael enjoying his job? What were the other wives like?

She answered, as enthusiastically as she could. She described the house and what she had done to it, with Susan nodding her approval, and she passed on a few titbits about the other wives, which made Susan giggle conspiratorially.

And then she stopped. The waiter had brought two plates of guinea fowl breast and they began the delicate task of separating the small pieces of dark meat from the tiny bones.

She said: "I wanted to talk to you about something in particular. It's a bit of a problem, really."

Susan looked up, noticing the change in tone.

"You know you can talk to me. I'm listening."

She faltered, laying down her knife and fork, and told her, searching for the words to express the inexpressible.

"Michael . . . Michael doesn't pay much attention to me, you know. In fact, our marriage is a total failure in bed."

She watched her friend's expression. Susan blushed, but composed herself. She was shocked, though; she could tell it.

For a few moments neither said anything. Then, as between sisters: "Do you mean that he's not much good at it? Is that it? You know, a lot of men are like that to begin with. Between ourselves, Guy is a bit quick most of the time, all the time in fact. They don't un-

102

derstand . . . They can't help themselves."

She shook her head. "He's not even quick. He won't."

Susan was not prepared for this information, and stared, almost open-mouthed at her friend.

"He should see a doctor. Maybe he can't manage . . ."

"It's not that. I know he can manage. You see . . ." She paused. "I suppose I should spell it out. Before we married we didn't go the whole way, so to speak, but I know that he's capable . . ."

"So he doesn't want to? Never?"

"Never."

The topic broached, they talked about it freely. There were tears — she couldn't help herself — but the diners at the neighbouring tables noticed nothing. A handkerchief was passed, and a few minutes later she was able to go on. Susan touched her lightly on the wrist, and then held her hand lightly as the relief of confession flooded over her.

She explained that she could not talk to him about it, that he would leave the room if the subject came up, that he was just pretending that the problem did not exist. And as to whether she still loved him — yes, she did, although she felt frustrated and angry with him.

Then they talked about his suspected affair. Susan said that in her view it was likely.

"Men don't go without sex," she said. "They just don't. They carry on somehow. He may well be seeing somebody. Find out who it is."

Anne said: "I don't want to. I don't want to go into any of that. I just want to get him to take notice of me."

"Take a lover yourself. Show him. Force him to choose."

She was relieved that her friend had come up with the same solution; she felt endorsed. And Susan could help. She could arrange for her to meet somebody suitable — she knew scores of men in Bulawayo, single men. She and her husband were members of a club that had hundreds of single members. They could help her.

Dr Leberman said: "You know, you're in a very difficult situation. It's not simple to deal with a matter like this."

He looked at the doctor, momentarily irritated by his habit of passing his gold-topped pen from one hand to the other as he talked. They had drifted for over half an hour, he thought. And always the same, wandering discussions, the odd questions, the probing, the opaque hints.

"But that's what you're supposed to be able to do, isn't it?"

He regretted the tone of the remark, the petulance, and began to apologise, but Dr

Leberman waved the apology aside.

"Don't be embarrassed to speak. It's far better that you do. No, what I meant is that it is a very complex matter dealing with feelings of this nature. They go very deep in your personal psychology. Some people feel they need years of analysis."

"And do I?"

Dr Leberman smiled. "You might do, for all I know. I'm not a psychoanalyst, you see. I don't accept the *Diktat* from Vienna. All I can do is perhaps locate the problem for you and see if you can confront it yourself. Or, I suppose, to see whether you can work out how to live with it."

"And could you?"

The other looked up at his ceiling. He put down the pen. "I suspect that it would not be easy. You see, this is a matter of your psychosexual development, and those matters are very difficult to unravel. It's probably something to do with the way in which you responded to your earliest sexual urgings. But we would really have to delve into that at great length and even then I might not be able to help you. By the way, do you *want* to make love to your wife?"

It was not a question which had been asked before, and he found it difficult to answer. After the hesitation, though, the answer came out naturally.

"No. I don't."

It was against all his self-imposed rules, but Dr Leberman sighed.

"There you are," he said. "That's it. I could ask you why you married her in the first place, but I won't just yet. In the meantime, you should perhaps ask yourself whether you want me to do anything for you. I don't know if I can get you to desire women, you know. I might be able to help you to understand why you don't desire them — if it's true that you don't desire them — but I can't necessarily change what your real drives are."

"I don't seem to have any drives. Or at least, none of that sort."

"Are you sure? Everybody has drives, you know. They may just be suppressed."

He was silent, avoiding the doctor's gaze.

"I'm not aware of any. I don't seem to . . ."

Dr Leberman shook his head, almost angrily. "You are aware of them. You're denying them, that's all. You're denying them to yourself, and to me, if it comes to that." He paused, letting his words sink in. It was sometimes necessary to be frank, but one had to be careful. People were delicately constructed and you could pull the house of cards down if you weren't sufficiently circumspect.

"What are they then?"

It was the tone of challenge he had heard earlier on, and this was a good sign. He could engage him. And yet, if he told him what he thought, he would flee from it. He would be angry, perhaps genuinely hurt.

"I'd prefer you to think about them and tell me," he said quietly. "If I tell you what I think at this stage, I might upset you. I might be wrong. And anyway, it's better for you to reach an understanding of yourself by working through things on your own. I can perhaps guide you."

They had reached a temporary impasse. Dr Leberman looked at his watch, and Michael understood the signal. He rose to his feet.

"You'll want to see me next week."

Dr Leberman nodded, noting something in his diary.

"Think over what we talked about today. See if it makes you want to tell me anything. Maybe it won't. We'll see."

He left the building quickly, as he always did, hurrying down the front steps, his head lowered, so that nobody would recognise him. There were other reasons for being in there, of course, other reasons than the seeing of a psychiatrist, but for him only one name stood out on the board of neatly-painted doctors' names.

It was almost lunchtime, on a Saturday, and the town was closing down for the weekend. He walked to his car and opened the door. A wall of heat came out to meet him, and he waited a few moments before he eased himself on to the driver's seat. The steering wheel burned to the touch, but he would just have to tolerate that until he got moving.

There were no weekend duties for him at school, and so he was free. He could drive home and watch one of the cricket matches, or he could stay in town. He could have lunch, see a film, do anything. He felt free; he had escaped from Dr Leberman and his inquisition for the time being, and his time was his own. He could follow his drives, as Dr Leberman called them. He could do what he wanted. Why not?

He smiled at the thought. He would have lunch, go to the cinema, and then go to a bar. He could always find friends and have a drink with them afterwards. It could turn into an evening; he could stay in town.

He chose a film. It was cool in the cinema, and he relished the nostalgic smell of buttered popcorn and velvet that seemed to hang in the air of such places. He liked the darkness, the privacy of it; the temporary suspension of time and reality.

Then, afterwards, he left his car where he had parked it and walked up to the Selbourne Hotel. There was a bar there he went to occasionally and there were usually a few familiar faces. They were men he had nothing in common with; men who lived in suburban brick houses with mounted wooden propellers on the living room mantelpiece, the trophies of wartime service; real estate agents getting away from their families for an evening drink; divorced men with lines of care and disappointment around their eyes; bragging sportsmen. But there was an easy camaraderie amongst these men with their beer-bellies and their chain-smoking, and he found this comfortable. His background, and Cambridge, had taken him irretrievably beyond this, but this was the reality of Bulawayo.

He drank several beers, which made him feel mellow, comfortable. Then he left, walked back to his car, and drove out towards the railway station. It was dark now, and the streets had lit up. There were people about though, people strolling aimlessly, a few whites window-shopping, with a trail of bored children behind them; Africans on bicycles; fat rural women from the bush, chewing sugar cane, chattering to one another, children strapped on to their backs with wound cloth.

He slowed the car down, and then pulled into a parking place at the side. The street was unfamiliar to him, as it was away from the centre, and the shops here were for African trade. They sold blankets, bicycles, cheap cardboard suitcases. This was the land of the Indian traders, who stood at the doors chewing betel while their wives moved around inside, sari-clad, watching for shop-lifters and shrilly berating the black staff.

109

He got out of the car and began to walk down the street, looking idly at the cheap goods. Then, suddenly, she was at his side. She had emerged from a doorway somewhere, and he had not noticed her.

She said: "It's a nice night, isn't it?"

He looked at her. She was a coloured woman, but mostly white, he thought. She spoke with the nasal lilt which those people always had, a curious up-and-down tone.

He said: "It is. Yes."

She smiled at him. She had striking, handsome features, he noticed, but she had applied thick red lipstick, which spoiled the effect. They never knew where to stop; that was the trouble. There was too much flashiness.

"Are you doing anything right now?" she said. "Would you like a cup of coffee?"

He stopped. It was so direct, unexpectedly so, but he asked himself what he thought they would say. This was a nice way of putting it; an invitation, but in the form of a social suggestion. One couldn't take offence at this.

He turned and stared at her.

"I'm free," he said. "Where is your place? Is it close-by?"

She smiled encouragingly.

"Not far. Just round the corner. Actually, it's my sister's place, you see, but she's away. I look after it for her."

They walked in silence. He would have

liked to have said something, but he was not sure what he should say. She seemed not to expect him to speak though, and there was already a rather curious warm intimacy between them.

"Here we are. This is it."

It was exactly right. A low tin-roofed bungalow, with a strip of six feet for the garden to the front, a small frangipani tree, a verandah with two chipped iron chairs on it, a front door with a fly screen.

They went in.

"Sit in the lounge. I'll get the kettle on."

She disappeared down a narrow corridor and he went into the room she had indicated. It was small, petty, with a pressed-tin ceiling and a red-stone floor. There was the smell of the floor polish that was used for such floors — a heavy, waxen smell that reminded him of the school dormitories.

There were small signs of comfort. A table, with a lace tablecloth, a tattered green easy-chair, a bed with scattered cushions to make it look like a sofa. There was a framed photograph on a sideboard, a girl in a frilly dress, standing in front of the house.

He sat down on the sofa and looked up at the ceiling, at the fly-spots, at the decoration on the tin cornice.

"It's a nice place, isn't it?"

She was standing in the doorway, a cigarette drooping out of her mouth.

"It cost my sister a bomb," she said. "But it's a really beautiful house. Really classy."

He nodded. "It's nice."

She was staring at him.

"What do you do?" she asked. "Do you work on the railways?"

He smiled. "No. I'm a teacher."

She took the cigarette out of her mouth.

"A teacher? You're not joking are you?"

He shook his head. "Mathematics. Cricket."

"God."

There was a silence. She was still staring at him, but now she left the doorway and came into the room and moved over to the window and drew the curtains.

"Gives us a bit of privacy," she said. "You get all sorts of people outside, you know. People who won't pay for a ticket to the bioscope."

He watched her. She had taken the cigarette out of her mouth and stubbed it out in an ashtray. The ashtray was a stubby chrome model aeroplane on a spindly stand. The country was full of them.

She stood before him, her heavily-reddened lips parted, revealing white teeth.

"Do you need to learn anything, Mr Teacher?"

He watched as she unbuttoned her blouse and wriggled out of her jeans. She tossed her clothes aside, as if glad to be free of them.

"Like that, Mr Teacher? Like that?"

She crouched beside him and her hands were upon him, upon his chest. He could feel his heart; he could hear it. She laid her hands upon his chest, and then moved down and slipped her fingers under the waistband of his trousers.

"So, Mr Teacher. Lots to learn . . ."

"Don't . . ."

"Why not?"

"Just don't."

"You scared or something? Do you want something different? I know how to do lots of things, lots. You tell me. Don't be ashamed."

Her body was honey-coloured, long-limbed. For a moment he imagined that he could, that it might be possible, that with those honey limbs, that long body, that shape. But he closed his eyes.

"Could you pretend . . ." But he stopped.

"You've just got to tell me. Girls can act dirty too."

He rose to his feet, pushing her hands away lightly.

"I'll pay you," he said. "Here. Is this enough?"

She took the money and tucked it behind a cushion.

"You don't like me because I'm a coloured. Is that it?"

He shook his head. "Nothing to do with it. You're very beautiful."

"Then what's wrong?"

He turned away and started for the door. She watched him leave, and lit another cigarette, which she smoked naked, thoughtful, watching the smoke curl upwards to the ceiling.

She laid aside her book. The school was quiet; the half-term holiday meant that most of the boys were away, leaving only those who could not get home for whatever reason or who had had no invitation to stay with their classmates. Those left behind were often given small tasks to perform around the school or the houses, and won points for service in the elaborate competition of house standing.

So that boy was painting the generator shed near the house. He had been there since yesterday, she saw, and he was making slow work of it. She watched him from the verandah; he was clearly not enjoying the task. He was one of the senior boys, one who would be leaving that year. Why was he not at home? Divorced parents?

She picked up her book and read a few lines before putting it down again. The boy was standing back from the shed, contemplating his handiwork.

She stood up and walked over towards him.

"How's it going? I've been watching your

labours from the verandah."

He turned round and smiled at her.

"Slowly. Really slowly. I'm not a very good painter."

Her eye moved to the shed. "I can see that. Sorry."

He laughed. "I'm doing my best, I really am. It just all seems so . . . so uneven."

She looked at him. He was tall, and had a mop of fair hair; an interesting face. She had seen him before at school functions; noticed him. He stood out.

"Would you like a break?" she said. "I could give you something on the verandah. Cold lemonade maybe?"

"I'd love that," he said. "Thank you Mrs Anderson."

He followed her back towards the verandah.

"What's your name by the way?"

"Gordon," he said.

"Your first name?"

"James."

She suddenly felt reckless. "You don't have to call me Mrs Anderson, you know. It makes me feel . . . Just call me Anne."

She looked at him, meeting his eyes for a moment, and then she looked away.

"If you want me to," he said.

They talked as he drank the lemonade. He told her that his parents lived in Northern

Rhodesia and that it was too far for him to go for the half term. His father had a business in Lusaka and a tea estate up near Lilongwe, in Nyasaland.

"He wants me to run it when I finish with university," he said. "But I don't want to do that. It's so isolated. It's the middle of nowhere. I'd go mad."

"What do you want to do? Yourself?"

"I'd like to live somewhere like Cape Town or Johannesburg. I'd work for Anglo American. Run mines."

She thought of her own future. They might stay here forever, surrounded by the same people, the same tight, self-righteous community. What would there be to talk about down the years? How could she cope with emptiness?

"You're lucky," she said. "To be able to get away."

He looked at her sideways.

"I think of you as being luckier than me," he said. "I feel as if I'm in prison. You can get away. You can go off to Bulawayo when you want to. You can do anything you like. I can't even go beyond those gates without permission from my housemaster, and even then, where is there to go?"

She stared at him. She had never heard one of the boys talk like this before, but then she had never spoken to any of them, she thought. She had not thought of them as

116

people with longings, frustrations. They were just that amorphous mass, the boys. Now she was talking to a young man, not a boy.

"You hate it?" she said. "Is that what you're telling me?"

He was studying his hands, at the tiny splashes of paint on the tanned skin.

"I suppose so," he said. "I bear it. But I'd love just to get out more. I'd love to go off to Bulawayo now and then, just for a day. I feel so . . . so itchy."

She looked out past the pillars of the verandah. The sky in the distance was heavy, deep purple with rain. It was a sky that she loved; towering stacked clouds of water. There would be a storm, and already there was a warm wind, the first warning.

"I could take you into Bulawayo," she said. "You could come in with me."

He looked up sharply, and she saw the colour in his eyes.

"Could I? Really?"

"Yes," she replied. "Why not? Would anybody notice that you were away?"

"I could fix it," he said. "I could get one of the others to sign me in for afternoon duties. Nobody would be able to tell."

"Then why don't we go into Bulawayo?" she said. "I'm fed up too."

She noticed him hesitating and she guessed at the reason.

"My husband's away," she said. "He's gone

up to Salisbury to sort out next term's cricket away matches. Don't worry. He's not going to ask me what I'm doing."

That evening she ate her dinner alone in the dining room, listening to the radio. There was one of those endless political discussions that depressed her so: *I'm telling you that there is only one way forward in this country. Only one. We have to take the Africans into our confidence and show them that the Federation can be made to work and that there's something in it for them. This is partnership. We've simply got to recognise that there's no other way. If we keep denying them a part in the business of government, then that is going to lead to trouble sooner or later. Yes, I mean that. Riots. Stonings. It's no good running away from it. You can't turn the clock back, you know. The fact of the matter is that there simply isn't a British Empire to stand behind us any more; it's evaporated . . .*

She turned off the radio and sat before her half-empty plate. She felt uneasy, unsettled; as if she was brewing an illness of some sort. The storm had passed them by; perhaps that was it. The electricity in the air had not been discharged, but was still there, and she could feel it.

She pushed aside her plate, rose from the table, and went outside. The air was warm and heavy, scented by the arum lilies and the white flowers of the frangipanis. Above, the sky was a field of endless constellations dipping and swinging from black horizon to black horizon.

There were the lights of the staff houses; curtained squares, illuminated, and the lights of the school houses, dotted irregularly, some distance away. She walked out on to the path that led towards the school, regardless of the warnings Michael had given her of the dangers of snakes at night, especially in hot weather.

She approached the house, keeping back among the gum trees, which separated it from the playing fields. There was a smell of eucalyptus, which she loved, and dried leaves beneath her feet. This was his house, and he was there, although he said there were only five of them left in it over the break. She stopped, among the trees, not daring to go closer, to risk being spotted in the light from the windows. She saw that there was a light on downstairs, and several on the floor above. That was the common room, but it was empty. There was a table tennis table and a cupboard; chairs.

She waited. There was a rustling noise behind her and she started; a snake? But whatever it was had moved off, and there was silence. She turned back to look at the open window, and at that moment she realised why she felt uneasy, why she felt that something was wrong. She yearned to see James again.

She wanted him. She closed her eyes. It was impossible. She had to fight it. She could not allow it. But there was a feeling in her stomach, a wrenching, undeniable feeling. She wanted him.

She turned away, and walked back towards the house, through the night. She tried not to think about it, but she knew that she had already embarked on it and she could not stop. She would see him tomorrow. They would go to Bulawayo, as planned.

He came to the house the next morning, and she felt the same. He walked with her to the car, and they drove off, and she felt the same.

"I haven't asked you what you wanted to do," she said. "I thought that we could go for lunch at a place I know. The Orchard. It's on the Matopos Road. I've been there once or twice before."

"That would suit me," he said. "I don't care what we do. I just want to get out of here. By the way, I haven't got much money."

She laughed. "I'll take care of that. I've got plenty."

"I'm so fed up with the food we get here," he said. "Lunch somewhere else would be great."

They chatted as she drove in. He was an easy companion, a good conversationalist, mature beyond his years. She stole glances at him from time to time, and she felt her stomach lurch. I want to touch him, she said to herself. I want to touch this boy. What would he say? Would he be surprised if I were to lean over and put my hand on his arm, on his shoulder? Would he say: Look, I'm sorry, but . . . He would be shocked, of course. She was a married woman.

They arrived at the Orchard and they were led to the table which she had booked by telephone. It was a large restaurant at the back of an hotel; a paved area shaded under trellises with vines and grenadilla plants.

"This is great," he said. "It's a good choice."

The waiter appeared.

"I'm going to have wine," she said. "Would you like some too?"

He looked at her for a moment.

"It's against every rule."

"I know. That's why I asked you if you wanted some."

He relaxed. "Of course. Please."

She ordered, and a bottle of chilled white wine was brought to the table in a bucket of ice. The waiter poured them each a glass and then left them.

"This is very kind of you," he said. "I hardly slept last night, thinking about today."

It was a disclosure; she would tell him too. "Neither did I. I was looking forward to it as well."

Their eyes met, and searched, and she knew that they had each made everything plain. She reached for her glass, and took a sip, watching him. He looked away, and then back at her, and his lips parted slightly, as if he was about to say something.

She reached across, suddenly, and touched his hand, which was resting on the table. She felt him start, as if he had had a shock, but then, a moment later, his fingers brushed against hers and he pressed her hand briefly. Then he withdrew his hand and picked up the menu.

"You should order for me," he said. "I eat anything. You choose."

She looked at the menu.

"All right. I'll choose."

Then suddenly he said to her: "You're married . . . I . . ."

She looked up from the menu. "My marriage isn't working all that well, James."

He looked down at the tablecloth.

"I'm fond of Michael. It's just that sometimes people aren't suited to one another as husband and wife. It happens, you know."

He nodded. "I see."

"So don't let's talk about it."

They finished lunch and sat for a long time over coffee. It was almost four o'clock before they rose from the table. She told him that they would drive back straight away, so that his absence would not be noticed.

"I don't want to," he said. "I'd much prefer to stay here."

"So would I. But let's not court disaster."

"It'll come by itself," he said. "Disaster does, doesn't it?"

They drove back, largely in silence, but a comfortable silence. She hoped that they would not meet another car on the school road, as she did not want him to be seen with her. The road was quiet, though, and there was nobody.

She parked the car at the back of the house and he got out. It was now dusk, and here and there lights had been turned on.

"I should get back," he said.

She stopped him, and touched his hand.

"Not yet. Come inside."

She led him into the house, which was in semi-darkness, and he followed her through the living room and corridor to the spare bedroom. Mutely, she took him in and closed the door behind them. Then she turned round and put her arms about him, and slipped her hand beneath his collar.

She took him gently, slowly, to the bed, and they fell upon it, wordlessly. His skin was soft to her touch; so smooth; his breath came in short bursts, from excitement.

"Let's run away," he said. "Let's leave."

He held her to him, his hands against her back, warm.

"Go away? Where?"

"Anywhere."

"We could go down south. To Cape Town maybe."

She laughed. "And do what?"

"Live together," he said. "I get money from my grandfather's will when I turn eighteen. If we could last two months until then."

She kissed him, lightly, and pushed the hair back from his forehead.

"What a wonderful idea."

"So we can go? I could phone and tell my father I'm fed up with this place and I'm taking off for a while. I've only got a few more months here anyway — there's nothing to keep me."

"Let me think about it."

She lay back, with him in her arms, his skin warm against hers. He was eighteen, almost; she was twenty four. Six years. He was a boy still, though, and she was a woman. She imagined her father hearing the news; she imagined the scandal. And how long would it last? A few months, perhaps, until he got over the novelty of it and began to think about his future. No, she couldn't. She couldn't expect to tie him down, this beautiful boy, her plaything.

She said, suddenly: "It's late. You really must get back." And he arose from the bed, and dressed, and she glanced at him, at the last moments of precious, vulnerable nakedness.

She got up too, and stood before him.

Then she said to him: "James. When you go back tonight, don't be cross with me. I'm going to go away, but just by myself. So we won't see one another again. We can't. We just can't."

He protested, but she put her finger to his lips, and he became silent. Then she led him out of the house and watched him until he was swallowed by the darkness of the night.

She went back into the house and retrieved her suitcases from the wardrobe. She packed indiscriminately, mixing clothes, and papers, shoes, books. Then, when the suitcases were full, she dragged them out, one by one, to the car and manoeuvred them into the boot.

She closed the house, but did not lock it. Michael would be back the following evening and everything would be safe until then. He would be pleased, she thought. He would be relieved that she had solved the problem for him.

She got into the car and began to drive down the school road, going slowly for the bumps that came suddenly and unexpectedly. Going slowly, she saw him at some distance, standing in the roadway, waiting for her. She slowed to walking pace, and he walked out and stood before the car.

"I was waiting for you," he said. "I've got my bag over there."

He pointed into the darkness.

"Don't go without me," he said. "Please."

She turned off the car engine and doused the lights. He was leaning in at the window, and had reached out to touch her.

"I'm in love with you," he said. "I really am."

She smiled, but he could not see that, and there came into her mind the memory of him in her arms, and the moonlight through the window on his limbs, and the shadows of his body. And would it matter if it was only for a few months, or even weeks? She had seduced him; perhaps she owed him something.

He had opened her door now and was crouching beside her, his arms around her.

"It's going to rain soon," she said. "You'll get wet."

"I don't care," he said.

"Get your bag," she said. "Quick."

He released her and dashed off into the darkness. Shortly afterwards he came back and they started their journey. The storm broke, in great lashing torrents, and there was lightning, joining sky to earth in silver flashes. She said, her voice raised against the noise of the rain drumming against the car: "Will you always remember how it rained when we went away?"

He nodded. "Yes. I will."

FAR NORTH

She said to her friends: "I won't stay. It's just for a year or so. Then something will turn up here and I'll come back to Sydney."

They tried to be understanding and said: "It won't be so bad. We know someone who went up there and liked it a lot. We'll come and see you. We'll come and see the reef."

But she knew that this was the end. It would be humid — unbearably so — and she would pine for everybody. There would be no arts cinema (perhaps no cinema at all), no Italian restaurants, no bookshops open until ten at night. There would be men in shorts, with white stockings rolled up to just below the knee. Social life would revolve around barbecues, with steaks, and silences. It would be Australia boiled down, distilled.

Yet it was not quite like that. There was no arts cinema, but it was extraordinary how you didn't miss an arts cinema in the heat. And there *was* an Italian restaurant in town, but she found that she didn't want to go to it. And as for the men in the white stockings — they were there, but you had actually to go to the bars with stools before you saw them. And of course there was the sea, with its impossible, heartbreaking blues; and the coastal mountains, covered with impenetrable green; and beyond the mountains, the great plains, under mile upon mile of sky, all the way to the Gulf of Carpentaria. So she wrote to her friends, and said: "You know, I'm glad I came. I'm happy here. Do you believe that? No, you probably don't, but I am."

She was busy at work, which she enjoyed. She had only qualified two years previously, and she was still learning, but her new colleagues were helpful. It was sometimes not easy in building, as some men would be unaccustomed to a female quantity surveyor, but she knew how to deal with that. Some women felt obliged to resort to aggression to make the point; she simply chose to be competent. That usually worked.

She found no difficulty in getting a place to live. There was a small suburb of the town, poised on the edge of the hills, which appealed to her immediately, and she soon paid a deposit on a house which had been carved out of an old Queenslander bungalow. It had been badly converted, and the corners which had been cut were glaringly obvious to her professional eye, but this was taken account of in the price. She could take out the cheap plumbing later and get rid of the yellow bath. In due course she could remove the mock-Venetian light fittings from the sitting room and find something old. It would not be difficult.

Within two months, she had made an impression on the house, and she felt that it was acquiring again some of the character that had been wrenched out of it by the developers. She felt quite at home now, and she decided that she would hold a house-warming. She had made a few new friends, and there were the people at work too. There were the makings — just — of a party.

As it happened, she need not have worried about numbers. Guests brought their friends, and some of the friends brought their own friends. In Sydney this could have caused resentment, but here it seemed to be welcomed. She found herself showing the yellow bath and the formica kitchen to people she had never met, and, outside, round the barbecue, somebody even asked her to introduce her to the hostess.

The house-warming party proved to be the beginnings of a social life. She found that she was invited to several parties the following week, and these led to further invitations. It was all very relaxed and informal, and she liked it. Then, one Sunday evening, she was telephoned by Bill Jameson, a construction engineer who worked in another department of the office. She had hardly even met him; she had invited him — along with everybody from the firm — to the house-warming, but he was in Brisbane that weekend and had been unable to come. She had heard little about him and their paths had not crossed professionally, but there seemed no reason why she should decline his invitation to drive up the coast the following Saturday.

"We could have lunch up in the Daintree, or somewhere round there," he said. "We'd be back in Cairns early evening."

She accepted, but took the precaution of saying that she had something lined up for that night and would have to be back by six at the latest. She liked a let-out, just in case. If Bill Jameson turned out to be all right, then perhaps they could have dinner somewhere. Perhaps.

It started badly. At about the time he was expected, she was in the kitchen. She heard a car hooting outside, and looked out of the window. It was him. She waved from the window, and he acknowledged her, but still he stayed in his car. It wouldn't have been too great an effort, she thought, to get out of the car and walk the six steps to the front door and her door bell. Still, let's be charitable; it is pretty hot and he's probably got the air-conditioning on in the car.

He did. She sat back, enjoying the cool as they drove along the road that led north. He said very little as they drove out of town, but then he began, and she realised immediately that she had made a terrible mistake. She did not like Bill Jameson. She knew intuitively

that she would disagree with his entire out-
look — on everything — and she also ob-
jected to his talking about fishing. Nor did
she take to the way he talked about sharks.
What was wrong with sharks, she wondered?
If you don't like them, then you shouldn't go
swimming. Sharks were, after all, perfectly
avoidable.

"You can't reason with a shark," said Bill
Jameson. "Carry a knife with you in the
water, always. If a shark gets too close, go for
its nose, right there, straight in. Sharks don't
like that."

"They don't?"

"You bet yours they don't," confirmed Bill.
"Would you, especially if your guidance
system was in your nose?"

He seemed to wait for an answer, which
did not come. He glanced at her, and then
continued: "Do you know the biggest shark
caught out there? It was a great white — a
massive thing. I forget how big, actually, but
pretty big. It could eat a boat. Now a reef
shark's different, quite different."

She made an effort, but not a very strenuous one. "Oh yes?"

"Yes. A reef shark is a fairly . . . a fairly
liberal sort of shark." He chuckled at his
choice of adjective. "It won't go for you if
you keep out of its way, and even then it will
back off. They always back off. Always."

"Have you ever seen one?" she asked,

looking at the cane fields and the heat haze.

"A reef shark? Yes."

"Did it back off?"

He was silent for a moment. "Not exactly. It was in a tank, actually. It didn't have much room."

She turned her head back to the cane fields and grimaced. It was ten o'clock now. There were eight hours to six o'clock — could she bear it? When she was a child and obliged to sit through something tedious, she remembered praying for a natural disaster to occur. If only there'd be a storm, or an earthquake, or a freak bolt of lightning, then the ordeal would come to a premature end. She remembered doing this in church, as she sat though the long-drawn-out sermons and the rituals, willing the arrival of the moment the priest said: *The peace of God which passes all understanding* . . . And her heart would give a leap at the impending release from durance vile. But before then, the only salvation would lie in natural disaster, or sudden death, which never occurred when they were wanted.

Perhaps the car would break down and they'd have to go back to Cairns by bus. Perhaps the bus would be virtually full, with one seat in the front (for her) and one seat in the back (for him). She would find herself seated next to an interesting man or woman, who, by way of introduction, would say: "I hate fishing, don't you?"

"Barramundi," said Bill. "That's a fish for you. Have you ever seen one? No, I don't suppose you have. You're new up here. What fighters! They get the lure between their teeth and they'll drag you for miles before they give up. Fantastic fish!"

She imagined how the conversation might progress: *"Have you ever got one, Bill?"*

"Yes, of course."

"And did it put up a good fight?"

"Well, it was in the fishmonger's actually . . ."

On the landward side of the road, the cane fields had given way to thick jungle, and on the other there were cliffs crumbling down to the sea. She looked out towards the reef, but thought only of fish, so she turned towards the jungle and studied that. There were one or two houses built up on the hillsides, half-hidden by greenery, and she thought of how it would be to live somewhere like that, tucked away from everyone, with just the jungle sounds to disturb you. What would you do? How would you pass the time?

For an awful moment, she thought of being stuck in such a place with somebody like Bill. How long could she bear that? She would murder him, she thought. She would push him over a cliff, or into a ravine, or put a western taipan into his bed. And it would be entirely understandable. The jury would sympathise and acquit her on one of the new defences to murder: cumulative provocation, or battered woman syndrome, or even pre-menstrual tension. Women were allowed to kill men now, but only if they deserved it, of course.

Bill said: "Now, let's work out what we're going to do. There's a very good place for lunch up there. I know it well. A fish place. Would that suit you?"

She nodded glumly. Perhaps I could drink a whole bottle of wine, she thought. That would anaesthetise me. Or there might be an earthquake . . .

"Then," Bill went on, "It's just occurred to me that we could go over to the crocodile farm. You aren't a real Northerner until you've seen a few of those creatures at close range. How about it?"

"A tremendous idea," she said. Then added: "Is there an arts cinema up here?"

Bill looked puzzled. "An arts cinema? No, I don't think so. Why should there be?" Then, almost suspiciously: "Why do you ask?"

"Oh, just interested," she said. "I was just wondering."

Bill smiled. "If you want to go to the cinema, I can take you. There's one in Cairns, you must have seen it. I can take you there, if you like. I'll have a look at the programme. I think they show arty films from time to time."

Her heart sank. "No," she blurted out. "I

mean, thanks very much. I just wanted to check and see if there was one. I never go. Ever."

They ate their lunch in almost total silence. She felt guilty about this, as he was being kind to her, and he couldn't help being what he was, but she found that she just could not summon up the energy to engage in conversation. Besides, she did not want to encourage him, and if he thought that she was boring, then that would be perfectly all right by her. She was dreading a further invitation from him — if he was planning one — as she knew that the only thing to do would be to decline immediately and unambiguously. She could invent a steady partner somewhere else — but that always seemed like cowardice to her. It was better surely to be honest, even if it caused some degree of hurt.

She imagined saying: "Bill, I'm sorry to have to say this, but I'm just not interested in fishing. You deserve somebody who knows about fish, you really do. There are plenty of women interested in fish, plenty. You'd be wasted on me. You'll find somebody."

How would he react? He would probably not take the hint.

"You could learn about fishing. I'll teach you. Look, I've got quite a few books that start from the beginning. I'll lend them to you."

It was undoubtedly better to be honest, if the occasion arose. Still, dishonesty could involve some amusing possibilities. She could try saying:

"Bill, I'll tell you straight out. I'm a lesbian. Lesbians and fishing just don't mix — believe me." She felt sleepy after lunch, and actually dozed off in the car on the way to the crocodile farm. She awoke as they arrived, feeling slightly better, and even quite interested in the long, low buildings in front of them.

"The crocodile farm," announced Bill. "Hundreds and hundreds of potential handbags walking around growing bigger by the moment. Quite a thought, isn't it?"

He was adept at destroying her interest in a subject, and the crocodile farm suddenly seemed less attractive. Yet, it was an experience, she supposed, and you couldn't see these places anywhere else.

They went inside. There was a large lobby into which every visitor was directed, and this was filled with crocodile memorabilia of every sort. There were crocodile oven gloves, crocodile tee-shirts with smiling, caricatured reptilians boxing, or dancing, or in one particularly offensive case, making love. There were crocodile key rings and crocodile balloons. There was something for everyone, provided one's taste was appropriately low.

Bill was delighted, and swiftly bought a

crocodile-skin wallet and a passport holder which announced, in gold lettering: *Citizen of Godsown.* She waited for him as he made his purchases, and admired his choice. Then he gave her the passport holder.

She was aghast.

"But I'm not going anywhere," she stammered, staring at the offensive object. "It's terribly kind of you, but shouldn't you keep it? You go off to Singapore from time to time, don't you."

Bill nodded. "But I've already got one," he said.

There was no escape, and she thanked him, tucking the present into her hip pocket. Perhaps it would fall out before she got back into the car. Then later on it might be found by somebody who would really appreciate it. She looked around her. Everybody in the lobby looked as if they would be delighted with it. Well, somebody would be in luck.

"Don't mention," said Bill. "Now let's go and take a look at the walking handbag department."

There was much to see. In a large display corridor the entire life cycle of the crocodile was displayed, from the moment of hatching onwards to pictures of bleached crocodile bones in the detritus of a dry river bed. There were clusters of eggs in an incubator, and small crocodiles, no bigger than a man's hand, but even at that stage quite capable of removing part of such a hand in their needle-like teeth. There were pictures of crocodiles eating and sleeping, and, in one shocking display, mating.

"Geez," said Bill, peering closely at the photograph. "Look at that! Look at his . . . his you know. Isn't it disgusting!"

She averted her gaze. "Just like the human male's," she muttered under her breath.

"What was that?" Bill asked sharply. "What did you say?"

But she had started to read from an explanatory leaflet. "The Estuarine, or Saltwater Crocodile, is the largest, and most aggressive of the crocodile family. It lives in rivers along the northern coasts of Australia, although there have been reports of rare individuals being spotted several hundred kilometres out to sea. Its prey include turtles and fish, and, occasionally, human beings who are unwise enough to enter its habitat. Each year in Australia, several people lose their lives in crocodile attacks."

"You can say that again," said Bill. "There was a chap in the office, you know, who knew somebody whose brother was taken while fishing. He got too close to one of them, and, whoosh, it got him. They're fine, though, as long as they're not hungry. It's when they're hungry that you've got to look out."

She said nothing. His remark, she thought,

added little to her knowledge of crocodiles. But now they moved on, past a family with bored-looking children and harassed parents, out into the open part of the display, where the live crocodiles lay, basking in the sun.

The crocodile farm was well laid out. The visitor could move about, from pen to pen, and see crocodiles in various stages of development. There were other animals, too, a pen of wallabies and some kangaroos, and a cageful of brightly-plumaged birds. But the star attraction was an enclosure tucked away in a corner where a crocodile, claimed to be the largest crocodile in captivity, could be inspected.

This pen was fairly large. In order to allow the visitor to inspect the occupant, a raised cement walkway had been constructed over one part of it, so that people could look down, directly into the crocodile's domain, which consisted of a largish, very muddy pool and several sand banks. "Old Harry" said a notice, "The largest croc under lock and key. Thought to be about forty years old."

They made their way on to the walkway and looked down. Old Harry was some way away, at the other end of the pen, lying on a bank, his feet splayed out, his eyelids closed. There were several flies buzzing about his flared nostrils, and one or two crawling around the moist edge of his eyelids.

They stared at Old Harry for a few minutes, both of them fascinated by the sheer immensity of the creature.

"Now, that's a croc for you," said Bill, his voice awed.

She nodded, in spite of herself.

"Yes."

They turned away, to retrace their steps down the walkway, and as she did so, she felt something catch against the rails. She turned round, wondering whether she had snagged something against a wire, and saw, spiralling the ten feet to the sandbank below, her passport holder.

For a moment, she wanted to laugh, but checked herself.

"Bill," she said. "Something terrible has happened. Look!"

Bill came over to her side and looked down.

"Oh no! Your passport holder!"

She smiled. "Well, I appreciated the thought, I really did."

He was frowning. "We can't leave it there," he said. "It cost twenty four dollars."

She shrugged. "I'm sorry, but I'm not going down there to fetch it."

He looked down again, and then looked over to the other side of the pen. Old Harry was unmoving, his eyes still firmly closed. He seemed quite unaware of their presence and could, for all intents and purposes, have been dead, and stuffed.

Bill straightened up. "I'll go down and get it. That chap over there is fast asleep and has probably already had his tea. I can climb down here quite quickly."

"Don't," she snapped. "Don't be so stupid. He could wake up."

"If he does, then I'll just scale right back up," said Bill, already beginning to clamber over the fence that ran down the side of the walkway.

She reached out and caught him by the shirt, trying to stop him, but he brushed her off. She reached out again, and grabbed his arm, but once again, he pushed her off, and began to climb down the struts of the walkway.

"Tell me if you see him moving," he called up. "Discretion is the better part of valour!"

He had now reached the bottom. The passport holder was only a short distance away, on the sandbank, and he moved gingerly towards it. She looked over towards Old Harry. He still seemed to be soundly asleep although, for a tense moment, she thought she saw an eyelid flicker. But it was only a fly, she decided.

Bill reached down to pick up the passport holder. Then he straightened up and waved it up towards her, in triumph. The gold lettering of *Citizen of Godsown* flashed in the sunlight.

The muddy water of the pond erupted in a great heave as the great shape of the second crocodile, Old Harry's companion, launched itself towards its prey. For a moment all she saw was teeth and an expanse of pink-white flesh within the mouth, and then the jaws clamped tight, with a crunch, around Bill's legs.

Bill looked up in outrage. She saw the passport holder waving, and she tried to scream, but no sound came. The jaws opened again, and then closed and moved backwards. Bill disappeared under water amidst a turbulence of bubbles and foam. Then the surface of the water settled.

Old Harry, in the meantime, opened his eyes, looked over at the pond, and then closed his eyes again and went back to sleep.

For a few moments she was too shocked to move. Then she heard shouting, and a man was running over to the pen. He was wearing a wide-brimmed hat and was carrying something in his hand — a stick, a gun, she could not see.

"What's going on?" the man shouted at her. "What's happening?"

She opened her mouth, but could not speak. She pointed at the surface of the water and then she screamed.

The man spun round and peered into the pen.

"Oh my God!" he muttered. "Is there somebody in there?"

"I told him not to go . . ." she began.

The man had moved away now and was

struggling with the lock on a gate. He stopped after a moment, and peered into the enclosure. Then he brought the gun up to his shoulder and there was an explosion.

Old Harry shot up and slithered down his bank with extraordinary speed. The man swore, loudly, and fired again into the water. There was movement of some sort, and a further commotion. Another shot, and then silence.

There were others on the walkway now. A man in a green uniform had arrived, and was shouting at people to keep clear. Then somebody took hold of her hand and led her away. She tried to resist, but the man with the gun was gesturing towards a building a little bit away and they took her there. Inside, a woman wearing a small gold crocodile badge sat her down on a chair and held her hand. They brought her tea, but her shaking hands spilt it over her jeans and blouse. They brought a cloth and dabbed at the hot stains.

"It's terrible," said the woman. "Was that your . . . your husband?"

She shook her head. "No. Just a friend. Not somebody I knew very well."

The woman seemed relieved. "Thank God for that," she said. "I don't think they're going to get him out."

It was some time before the man with the gun returned. He looked at the woman, who exchanged a glance with him.

"It was a friend of hers," she said. "Not somebody she knew well."

The man's expression lightened.

"That's something," he said. "Well, I'm very sorry to have to tell you that he was taken by that crocodile. Right down the hatch. There was nothing we could do, but I've shot it and they're hauling it out at the moment. Did he climb in?"

She nodded. "I tried to stop him, but he wouldn't let me. He didn't know there was another crocodile under the water."

The man grimaced and flung the rifle down on a table.

"This is the first bloody time it's happened," he said. "I knew it would, sooner or later. Some damn joker would take his chances."

"Watch it, Pete," said the woman. "This lady's upset."

"I'm sorry," he said. "It's a terrible thing, I know. I've called the police, by the way. They'll want to know exactly what happened. Can you tell them all right? Make sure that you tell them that it was nothing to do with our fences — that he climbed in. Okay?"

She felt calmer now, as the first effect of the shock began to wear off. It was overwhelming, terrible, but it wasn't her fault. She tried to stop him. There was nothing she could have done; she had no need to reproach herself. And yet the memory of her lack of charity came back to her with awful clarity, and she shuddered at the recollection.

The police arrived shortly afterwards. She became aware of their presence through the sound of the sirens, and then, some twenty minutes later, a sergeant came into the office. He exchanged a few murmured words with the other woman and then drew a chair over to where she was sitting.

"I'm very sorry about this, Miss," he began. "But I'm going to have take a statement from you."

She looked up at him. There was something about his tone which left her unsettled, something harsh and unfriendly. She saw too that his expression was one of barely perceptible distaste. Well, it certainly wasn't a pleasant matter, and these people must become tough in their job.

She gave an account of what had happened, stressing that she barely knew Bill Jameson.

"I told him not to climb in," she said. "In fact, I tried to prevent him, as I told the manager here. But he was determined to fetch that ridiculous piece of crocodile skin."

"The passport holder? Can you describe it?"

She gave him a description, and he noted it down, word for word in his notebook: Inscription: *Citizen of Godsown*. Then he looked at her expectantly.

"He climbed down into the pen and picked up the passport holder. Then, I think it was just a second or two later, a crocodile appeared from nowhere. It must have been underwater."

The sergeant nodded.

"How did you try to restrain him? What did you do?"

She closed her eyes. "I grabbed him by the arm. Then I think I got hold of his shirt."

She opened her eyes. The policeman was staring at her, unblinking.

"You didn't shout for help?"

She was puzzled. "When he was trying to climb in, or later when he was in the pen?"

"When he was climbing in."

She paused before answering. Should she have done more than she had? Was this man suggesting that she had failed in some way — that it was her fault? She felt a prickle of irritation within her. This was ridiculous. Bill had brought the whole matter upon himself by his own stupidity. She could hardly have done more to stop him without falling in herself.

The policeman was drumming his fingers on the table, as if impatient for an answer.

"No," she said. "It all happened very quickly. I didn't have time to think. I just tried to stop him."

"Very well," said the policeman. "So you didn't shout for help."

"No."

"Don't you think it would have been a good idea? There were people not far away. They might have come and helped you to stop him."

Her irritation returned. He was now making the allegation more directly.

"I've just told you," she said, her voice rising in anger. "It happened very quickly. I didn't think about shouting — I just thought about stopping him physically. And I couldn't."

The policeman sat back in his chair and toyed with his pen.

"You didn't by any chance push him, did you?"

Push him! For a moment she was too astonished to say anything. Then, when she responded, her voice was tiny, almost inaudible.

"Do you think I pushed him in? Actually pushed him?"

The policeman smiled. "It's a possibility, isn't it?"

Now she knew that he was taunting her, and anger replaced irritation.

"Well, that's a stupid joke. I've just witnessed something pretty terrible and you think you can sit there and joke about it."

The policeman stopped smiling. "It's not a joke, stupid or otherwise. I happen to have grounds for my suggestion, and you'd better take it damn seriously. Understand?"

She looked over his shoulder to the woman

who had given her tea. She looked away, as if to say: leave me out of this. But she could tell that she was enjoying every moment of the drama.

"You see," said the sergeant, turning a page in his book, "I've just interviewed a child who was a little way along the path, heading towards the pen. He said to me — and I'll quote you his words if you like — 'The lady pushed that man into the croc's place. I saw her do it. She pushed him.'"

They drove her from the crocodile farm directly to the police station. A policewoman sat beside her in the back of the police car and accompanied her into a small office, where they sat together in silence. A few minutes later the sergeant returned with another policewoman who explained to her that she was going to take her fingerprints and take a further statement from her, if she wished to give one.

She was too shocked to be anything but compliant. Her hand was limp as they inked each finger and pressed it against the sheet of paper. Then they carefully wiped each finger with a moist tissue, and wrote something on the sheet.

"You can speak to a lawyer if you like," said the sergeant. "I've got a list of lawyers in the area, and you can telephone one of your choice. Do you understand?"

He handed her a piece of paper and she pointed to one at random. One of the police-women offered to dial the number for her and she spoke a few words before handing the receiver over to her. The lawyer sounded friendly, and promised that he would be at the police station within the hour. She put the telephone down. The sergeant was looking at her.

"Why did you push him? You can tell us the truth, you know. It's always, always easier that way, I promise you."

Later, alone with the lawyer, in a different room, he said to her:

"The problem as I see it is this. They've got a statement from this eight-year-old boy to the effect that he saw you pushing him in. Apparently he's adamant about it and is sticking to what he said at the beginning. He said that he saw the man hit you and then you pushed him in."

He paused, watching her as she drew in a deep breath and shook her head in frustration.

"I take it that that's just untrue?"

"Of course it's untrue. I've told everybody what happened. Why would I push him into a crocodile pen? I hardly knew him."

"What was your relationship, may I ask? Did you like him?"

"No. I did not. He was . . . a bit of a

149

bore, I'm sorry to say. I wasn't proposing to go out with him again. It was just a casual date, as I've told you."

The lawyer pursed his lips. "I wouldn't say too much about not liking him, if I were you," he said, his voice lowered. "That could be misunderstood by a jury."

She stared at him in disbelief. He really thought that this was all being taken seriously, that the absurd misunderstanding of an eight-year-old was going to result in some sort of trial.

The lawyer continued. "The child's statement is inherently unreliable, of course. Children misunderstand things, and I've already established that the child was some way away at the time. He could easily have interpreted your attempts to keep Bill from climbing in as attempts to push him over the edge. But there's another problem."

"What's that?"

"This passport holder. The thing that he went into the pen for. They can't find it. They've opened up the croc that took him, of course, and the stomach contents have been listed. No passport holder. They've also drained the pond, and it's not in the mud. So where is it?"

She shrugged her shoulders. "I haven't a clue. Anyway, why does that matter?"

The lawyer sighed. "It matters, I'm afraid, because if there's no passport holder, then a valuable element in the corroboration of your story is missing. Do you see that?"

She looked down at the floor. She could not quite decide whether the lawyer believed her or whether he was on the sergeant's side. If he didn't believe her, then she wondered whether she could convince anybody. She imagined the jury, twelve solid citizens of Godsown, staring at her in disbelief as she explained about a vanished crocodile skin passport holder. She remembered the dingo case. They hadn't believed her either.

The lawyer left just after seven in the evening, promising to return the next morning. A different policewoman had appeared now, and told her that she was being held without charge, pending a police decision as to proceedings. There was nothing she could do about this, she said, and she might as well settle down for the night. She would have to share a cell with another female prisoner, and they would provide her with night clothes and a reasonable "quantity of toiletries". She could make another phone call if she wished, to notify anybody of her "continued presence in the police station". That was all.

She went mutely to the cell, where she saw another woman lying on a bed, reading a magazine. The woman did not acknowledge her presence until the door was closed again and the policewoman had gone. Then she laid down her magazine and smiled at her. She saw a thin woman in her late thirties, with a pinched, trouble-lined face.

"What they got you in here for?" asked her cell-mate.

"Pushing a man into a crocodile pen," she said. "What about you?"

"Shot me old man," she said cheerfully. "Just once. Didn't finish him off, and he's back in the pub by now I expect."

"Shot him? Why?"

The other sat up on her bed and reached for a packet of cigarettes from her bedside table.

"He bloody asked for it, he bloody did." She lit a cigarette and exhaled a cloud of acrid smoke. "He clouted me regular. He clouted the kids too. He's bad news."

She took another drag of her cigarette. "And another thing. Pretty funny, come to think of it. I shot him in the stomach with my son's .22 rifle and made a neat little hole. And do you know, beer poured out of it, I swear to God it did! He was full of beer and it came straight out in a little jet, just like he was a barrel with the bung taken out!"

She slept well, in spite of everything, after chatting with her new-found friend until late at night. Then, shortly after eleven in the morning, the lawyer arrived. She was taken to the interview room to await him and he came in smiling.

"Good news," he said. "Old Harry died."

She looked at him in astonishment.

"Old Harry, the other crocodile in the pen. It seems that he died of a broken heart. That was his mate they shot, you see. Apparently Old Harry just turned up his toes and snuffed it."

She began to wonder whether she had made a mistake in her choice of lawyers, but he continued. "The vet opened Old Harry up this morning, just to be on the safe side. And they found that he was a citizen of Godsown, believe it or not."

She allowed herself to laugh, cautiously at first, but with an overwhelming feeling of relief as the lawyer went on.

"There must have been some sort of general commotion under water and Old Harry ended up swallowing the passport holder. He must have been after a bit of Mr Jameson. Anyway, the police are satisfied that this corroborates your story, and the young boy apparently seems less than one hundred per cent certain this morning that you actually pushed Mr Jameson in. In fact, he said this morning that he thought Mr Jameson may have been trying to push you in, but slipped in the process!"

She looked at the lawyer, seeing him for the first time as a man.

"I'll drive you back to Cairns if you like," he said. "I've got business to do there so it won't be any trouble."

They drove back slowly, even stopping to admire the view at one point. The sea was calm, and a small fishing boat was ploughing its way across the field of blue.

"You know," she said to him. "I don't really like fishing. I really don't. What about you?"

He looked at her, and smiled, knowing that his answer would be extremely important.

"No," he said. "I don't either."

INTIMATE ACCOUNTS

I am not at all sure whether I should be telling you this. My difficulty is that this is a grey area of professional ethics, and, quite frankly, no definitive guidance is available. Of course every doctor is subject to the usual rules of confidentiality — which are exceptionally strict — and this means that one should say nothing about what passes between psychiatrist and patient. So one simply could not telephone a patient's wife, say, and tell her what her husband had just revealed on the couch, tempting though that may sometimes be. That would be a clear breach of professional ethics and the medical authorities would raise a song and dance. And rightly so.

But it's by no means clear what the rules are when it comes to writing in a general way about what has happened in the consulting room, especially when there is no mention of names — or when false names are used. If one doesn't say anything that gives away the actual identity of a patient, then has any confidence been breached? The answer to this must be that if there is good reason to reveal — in this anonymous way — what has passed between analyst and patient, then one is doing nothing unethical.

Yet is there good reason for my telling you what follows? After a great deal of deliberation, I have decided that there probably is. I know that these are not the pages of a professional journal, where there would be every justification for the publication of case histories. I know, too, that some will be reading this in the wrong spirit — in a prurient way perhaps — but others (I hope most) will be reading this because they have a real interest in human nature. It would be professional arrogance of the worst sort if psychiatrists were to decline to speak about the more curious interstices of the human mind. The workings of the human psyche are not our exclusive preserve: Freud's essays, and the other classics of our craft, should be read by all. They are wonderful, liberating documents — profound literature, in fact. And if they are suffused with sexual matters, that is simply because human life itself is suffused with sex. There is nothing abnormal in wishing to understand how this affects the way in which we live.

Of course there is a great deal that is surprising in this part of people's lives. Nobody leads the narrow sex life which restrictive notions of normality impose on us; the human mind is too imaginative for that. Even the most unimaginative — the dullest — have their fantasies (dull fantasies perhaps), although very few confess them. And there is nothing inherently wrong in fantasy — as long as it remains fantasy and does not intrude upon reality. For most people the dividing line is quite clear; for others the distinction between the world of the imagination and real life becomes blurred, and it is at that point that behaviour becomes bizarre or inappropriate. Such cases are really very difficult to deal with, as the hold which a fantasy exerts may be very strong. I have had patients in therapy for years, struggling to obliterate some deep-rooted, troublesome fantasy, but failing, again and again.

In my calling I am exposed to everything, and nothing shocks me any more. *Nihil humanum mihi alienum est* or, to use the demotic, I am surprised by nothing. I don't say this to intimidate, or to suggest professional superiority; but it is nonetheless true. I have heard things which you simply would not credit.

But that is all by way of introduction. My real purpose is to talk about dating, which is an extraordinarily important and almost universal aspect of human life. Consider the word itself. For some it is an Americanism which is best avoided unless you happen to be an American. I am not. I am an Australian, but still I disagree. What are the alternatives? Seeing somebody? Going out together? These all sound rather coy to the modern ear. Dating is better.

Dating is patently a courtship ritual, and yet we very rarely see it as that. We acknowledge that courtship rituals are performed in other cultures; we identify them in other ages, in other species; but dating we take for granted, failing to realise just how significant it is. Dating is extraordinarily important: terrible things can happen on dates — *traumatic things* — which can trouble people to the very depths of their psyches. It is this insight which prompted me to record particular cases which I have encountered where something happens on a date to reveal some personal pathology, or where the date itself has a pathological effect. I discovered to my surprise that the pathology is extensive — one only has to be on the alert to spot it and expose it, layer after painful layer. Dating is the cause, and symptom, of great distress.

A major difficulty with our theoretical understanding of dating is that we simply do not appreciate the purpose of the entire encounter. If we see it for what it really is — a courtship ritual — then we can identify the deep structures of the ritual, and that enables us to detect what is really going on. So dating is really all about sex. In the conventional context, this means that the man invites the woman to go through a social encounter, the ultimate purpose of which is sexual engagement. It is most important, though, that this engagement does not occur too early. Attitudes, of course, have changed over the years, and the old question: "How far should one go on the first date?" strikes the modern generation as being charmingly old-fashioned. Yet the timing of an involvement is still important, and it can be very disturbing for both parties if things go too far, too quickly, as happened in the following case.

G consulted me after he had suffered a non-accidental injury in the course of a date. He was slapped by the woman, who dislocated and fractured his jaw. G required substantial treatment from a dental surgeon, which was particularly unfortunate, as in due course he revealed a morbid dread of dentists. This led him to assault the dentist, who fortunately was very understanding and agreed to let the matter rest, provided that G agreed to seek psychiatric help.

I suspected that the apparent dental phobia was displacement, and that the fear of dentists really masked a further, more difficult problem which had revealed itself in the dating behaviour. In other words, I wondered: why had the woman slapped him so hard? Here, I felt, we would find the key to the problem.

At first, G seemed reluctant to talk about the original episode, and kept coming back to the issue of his fear of dental pain.

G: But can't you see? That's what's really

worrying me. I don't see that it matters how I broke my jaw. It's what happened afterwards. I'm frightened of dentists.

Self: Of the dentist or the needle? Or of the drill, and the pain it brings?

G: I just don't like dentists.

Self: I don't think that is really what's worrying you. Let's return to the date. What happened?

G: What about the date? I took her out. Then she slapped me. Hard. My jaw was dislocated and two teeth became loose. Then all these dentists got involved.

Self: I suggest that we don't talk about dentists. I'd like to go through the events of that evening, one by one. You went to collect her from her flat. Start from there.

G: All right. If you insist. I went to collect her from her flat. She lived on the fourth floor. I rang the bell and she answered the door. I'm just about ready, she said. Come in.

So I went in. Her flat was very attractive, very feminine. It made me feel excited just to be standing there, while she went through to her room to collect her coat. Then she came out and we left, by the front door.

Self: And you were still excited?

G: Very. But I don't think it showed. Anyway, we went to my car, where I opened the door for her and then went round to get into the driver's seat. I was thinking at the time: What a wonderful woman. This one really is nice — much better than the last, *who only went out with me once.* Then I sat down in my seat and a few moments later, quite without warning, she slapped me and got out of the car. I drove straight to hospital. They looked at me, and took an X-ray of my jaw. They were very concerned about what had happened. *Then the dentists came.*

Self: But why should she slap you? Did you touch her in too familiar a way? Did you make an advance?

G: No, I did not! I never touched her at all. I just experienced a rather emotional moment. It was a physiological matter. That's all. I couldn't help it. Sitting there in the car, in such close proximity to her. It was all too much for me. This is not the first time it has happened. In fact, it happens on every date.

At the beginning of an encounter with a patient I usually find that I have a fairly shrewd idea of the general nature of the problem, but I had frankly not expected that this was one of those extremely rare cases of excessively premature ejaculation. Now that this was established, I was able to treat G with some success, using precisely those techniques which are appropriate when a man is embarrassed by *ejaculatio praecox*. The details of the treatment are irrelevant here, but it involved the conjuring up of mental imagery associated with non-sexual matters. I told him to think of something else when he next went on a date, and to keep that non-sexual image in his mind throughout the evening. This can't have been easy for him, but it was probably better than telling him to count. In any event, it worked reasonably satisfactorily — after one or two initial let-downs — and G, I believe, is now happily married. Married people don't need to go out on dates, and so his problem may be regarded as quite satisfactorily solved.

G's case is valuable in that it not only illustrates the fact that timing is still important, but also because it portrays a patient who told the truth in a quite disarming fashion. He did not *intend* to mask his real problem by talking about dentists: dentists were, in a way, the real problem — at least in so far as he saw it. When I pressed him on this, there was no attempt to conceal the cause of his social disgrace — on the contrary, he revealed it quite openly. It can be very difficult if a patient does not do this, and even more difficult if the patient is an out-and-out liar, as happened in the next case, that of Ms Ms.

It is very bad practice to allow oneself to dislike a patient, particularly to dislike her on first sight. This, I must confess, was how I felt about Ms Ms the moment she entered my consulting rooms. There was no question of my revealing it, of course, and so she would have had no idea how very distasteful I found her. I pondered my feelings for a moment while I read the referral letter written by her own doctor. *Don't trust this patient*, he had written. *Just don't trust her*.

We talked about her family for a while. I was prepared to take everything she said with a grain of salt, but most of it was, at that point, quite uncontroversial.

Ms Ms: I still see my mother and father regularly. They're retired now, and so they can come over for the weekend. They stay near me for a few days and we go on picnics — go out to dinner — that sort of thing. I don't really like going for picnics with my parents.

Self: Really?

Ms Ms: Yes.

Self: But even if you don't like the picnics,

you don't really feel anxious about them. It's just when you go out with a man? Is that it?

Ms Ms: Yes. I get terribly anxious.

Self: Why do you think that is? Have you had something unpleasant happen to you on a date? (*I wondered, at this point, whether she had been out with G, but that would have been too much of a coincidence.*)

Ms Ms: Yes. Precisely. It happened about two years ago. I was just twenty two then and I had not been out with men a lot. Anyway, I met this older man — or I put him into that category then. In fact, he was only about thirty, low thirties I think. I met him through a friend, and I thought that he was rather charming. It was at a tennis party, and I noticed that he was wearing long white trousers and a white sweater. It was quite warm at the time, and this struck me as a little bit odd, but perhaps he just felt the cold more than others. He was called M.

Self: Just M. Nothing else?

Ms Ms: Yes, I thought that a bit strange, too. I always think of M as a character in the James Bond books. But that's what he was called. Anyway, I didn't think much about him afterwards. In fact I didn't think about him at all until a week or so later, when he telephoned me.

M: It's M. You remember me? We met at Roger's tennis party?

Ms Ms: Oh yes, of course. How are you?

M: Fine, just fine. I wondered whether we could meet up some time. How about dinner?

We agreed to meet for dinner the following Friday. He said that he knew the chef at an Italian place and that it was probably the best restaurant in town. I said that I always ate ethnic and that I would expect him at eight.

We drove there in his car. I noticed that the car was rather unusual. It had a lever coming out of the instrument panel, and this ended with a curious handle. I couldn't help thinking about James Bond now, and I wondered whether this controlled an ejection seat and whether I should be *ejected prematurely.*

M didn't touch the handle on the way to the restaurant, and I did not like to ask him about it. He parked the car and we went in to the restaurant. As we did so, I noticed something about M which I hadn't noticed before. He walked in a remarkably stiff way — almost as if he was feeling the results of excessively strenuous exercise. In fact, he moved rather like a tin soldier.

The proprietor greeted M as an old friend, and was very polite to me. He kissed my hand, in an old-fashioned way, and made some compliment in Italian. Then he led us to the table and we sat down. Again, M's movements were rather stiff.

The dinner, as M had predicted, was wonderful. Then afterwards, over a glass of Sambuco and tiny almond cakes, M told me more about his life.

Self: I find that rather strange. People usually don't do that. They give a few facts, make a few brush strokes of the picture, but it's odd for somebody to tell another about his life.

Ms Ms: Well, he did. Why would I make it up? I've already told you that there was something unusual about him. M wasn't an ordinary sort of person. He simply wasn't.

Self: I'm sorry. I shouldn't have interrupted. Please continue.

Ms Ms: Well, he told me about his boyhood and how his father had been a well-known racing driver. He raced vintage racing cars — those funny old ones with bull noses — and he was very successful. He was a wonderful father for a boy to have, and M was proud of him.

M was sent off to boarding school, because his father believed in that sort of thing. M was unhappy there at first, as he was tormented by the other boys, who laughed at his name. Boys are like that, aren't they? Cruel — *just like men.* Then, one weekend, M's father drove up to the school in one of his vintage Bugattis and all the boys were terribly impressed. Now that they realised who M was, and what sort of father he had, they stopped teasing him. In fact, M was even cultivated by some of the older boys, who enquired whether they could come and stay with him during the school holidays. They wanted to drive a Bugatti, which is the sort of thing that most boys want to do. *Men, too.*

When M left school he went to university, but was asked to leave at the end of his first year. It was not that he could not have passed the exams, he told me, it's just that he had developed a passion for racing and he spent all his time on an old Bugatti his father had given him on leaving school. He wanted to get it into good enough order to race it, and that took over six months.

Then his first race came. He began to tell me about it, about how excited he was at the prospect, but then quite suddenly he stopped, and I saw that he was overcome by emotion. I knew that something awful had happened, and so I wanted to reassure him that he could tell me about it. I wanted to comfort him, as I have always found vulnerability in a man brings out my maternal instincts.

The table was very small, and I could easily reach out to M, which I did. I reached out and laid my hand on his leg, just above the knee. I meant to pat him, but I froze. My hand was laid upon metal. I felt overcome with embarrassment, and quickly transferred my hand to the other leg. That was metal too!

I suppose I should have stopped there, but it seemed to me that to stop at that stage would have been tactless. So I reached out for his forearm and touched it lightly. But even that light touch was enough to feel the pulleys of an artificial arm.

Now M looked up at me. "Yes," he said. "There was a terrible accident on that very first race. My two legs, my arms — both artificial. That's why I'm wearing white gloves."

I looked at his hands. It was extraordinary, but I simply hadn't noticed. M had a very strong face, you see, and my eyes had been held there.

Then M continued: "Not only that. Other bits of me are artificial too."

That was more than I could bear. Flustered, I changed the subject.

"Let's not talk about it any more," I said. "Let's talk about . . ."

"You," said M quickly. "Has anything ever happened to you?"

* * *

It was at this point that I made my diagnosis. I felt excited about it, as it was the first case of its sort in my own experience. *Confabulism*: Ms Ms was making everything up. M would not exist, or if he did exist, she would have totally distorted her encounter with him. There would be no car with a special lever — no Bugattis — and certainly no artificial limbs.

My intellectual excitement was mixed, though, with anger. The confabulist, who simply cannot resist making up stories, wastes an enormous amount of other people's time. I found that I resented being used by Ms Ms in this way, in much the same way as must those doctors feel who are tricked into providing elaborate operations for Munchausen's patients. How dare she sit there and spin me this story of this imaginary date!

Self: Let me stop you there, Ms Ms. This is all made up, isn't it? You're lying to me.

Ms Ms: Oh. Oh, so you can tell? Yes, I do tend to exaggerate a bit, I suppose. Some of what I say is true though . . .

The interesting thing about confabulism, of course, is what the patient's fables tell you about them. There was a reason why Ms Ms went to such trouble to construct the story of M. M, of course, could have been her father, and for some reason she wished to castrate him. As Freud has shown, that is quite a normal thing for a boy to want to do — indeed every boy wishes to castrate his father; it's perfectly normal — but why should a woman wish to do it? The clue, I think, lay in the name that Ms Ms had invented for herself. She wished to underline her status as a woman who didn't need men, and to do so had called herself Ms, and then doubled it. Not only that, but her desire to castrate went very much further than normal. It was a profoundly abnormal castration urge: she wanted to cut everything off — hands, arms and legs. What is more, she even shortened his name. This is what made her case so extreme.

But why did she want to emphasise her feelings of antipathy for men? The reason was self-evident: she had been badly treated by a man, and was playing out the hostility that she felt for all males as a result of this bad treatment. I was sure that if I delved more deeply into Ms Ms's background, I should find some boy or man who had spurned her, or let her down. It was probably not her father. I suspected that she liked her father because she had told me (untruthfully) that she did not enjoy going on picnics with him. It was some other male then. So I said to her:

"There was a boy in your life, some time

ago. You loved him. You loved him a great deal. But he didn't love you. He let you think that he loved you, but he didn't. You wanted him forever, because that's what women want — they want men forever — but this boy was only playing with you and he let you down. He went off with another girl. You didn't hate her; you hated him. You hate all men now. That's true, isn't it? Well, isn't it?"

She stared at me, pretending to be astonished.

"No," she said. "It isn't."

But I knew that she was lying.

If it would have taken some time to treat Ms Ms successfully, then how much longer would it have taken to deal with the third and final case I should like to recount — that of Big Hans. I choose this name for him to distinguish him from Freud's celebrated patient-by-proxy, Little Hans. The problem posed by Big Hans was one of personality disorder, which is always recalcitrant, and almost always beyond help. One cannot change one's personality — it is, to use a popular metaphor, the stack of cards dealt out in life which one simply has to accept.

Hans was the son of an Austrian immigrant, who had set up a chain of bakeries throughout Sydney and Melbourne and who had prospered greatly. He was his parents' only child — or so he thought — and he was given all the attention which such a position often attracts. In particular, his parents went to the trouble of bringing out from Austria a nurse called Irmgard, who smelled of starch, and strudel, and who embodied all the traditions of the Austrian nursery. Irmgard, who was in her early twenties when she arrived in Australia, was Tyrolean, and doted on Hans, or her Kleiner Hanslein, as she insisted on calling him.

Self: Irmgard was always there, you say? She attended to your every need?

Hans: Yes. She woke me up in the morning and gave me my bath. She spurned modern plumbing, and preferred to fill a large tin tub and stand it in the middle of the room. Then she took off my pyjamas and washed me all over with her special, sweet-smelling soap that she had sent out from home.

Self: And how long did this go on for?

Hans: Until I was eighteen.

Self: I see. Please continue. Tell me more about Irmgard.

Hans: She was very beautiful, and the photographs prove that this was really so and that it's not just my rosy memory of her. She had flaxen hair and a wonderful complexion. My mother used to say that Irmgard was *prachtvoll aus,* and that you would never find an Australian girl who had a skin like that. She warned Irmgard against the sun, with the result that I think she spent most of her time indoors.

After the bath, she dressed me. We would spend some time in front of my wardrobe, choosing what I was to wear that day. Irmgard was in charge of my clothing and she bought something new virtually every week. She had a sister who was a seamstress in Vienna, and she regularly sent out clothes which Irmgard had specially designed for me. She liked to dress me in an outfit of the style which Kaiser Franzi had worn when he was a child. It was full of buttons and cuffs, and we loved putting it on.

She made up little songs for me, one of which we called "The Dressing Song". It was partly in German — a pretty odd sort of German — and partly in English — she liked to play with English words, which seemed very strange to her ear. She had an excellent voice, and she taught me to sing too. I committed the words to memory before I knew their meaning, and I have never forgotten them. Here's one.

Mein kleiner Hans, Fancy pants!
Pretty Hans, King of France!
Oben-pants
Unter-pants —

    Let us dress
    Den Kleinen Hans!

Self: What about the other songs? Were they all along the same lines?

Hans: Yes, more or less. Some were better than others. I thought "The Dressing Song" was rather good, but my favourite was "The Bath Song". Would you like to hear the words?

Self: It could be helpful. In fact, I think these songs are really very important. I take it that you sang this particular song at bath time?

Hans: Yes. Evening bath time. Irmgard sang it.

    Kleiner Hans, mit seinem Scruggel
    Macht ein bischen Schmickel-Schmuckel;
    Naughty Billy, mit seinem Villy,
    Macht einen kleinen pantlich Hilly!

Self: An intriguing little song. But what about friends? Did you know many boys of your age?

Hans: Yes, quite a few. I used to get laughed at a bit, particularly when I was dressed up in my Kaiser Franzi outfit. In fact, when Irmgard took me for walks in the suburb in which we lived she used to carry a small imitation gun. When boys jeered at me, or laughed, she would pull this gun out of her handbag and point it at them. It gave them a terrible fright. Later on, she got hold of a starting pistol, and actually fired blanks at them.

Self: So you relied on Irmgard for protection?

Hans: Yes. But only until I was about six or seven. Then I worked out a way of looking after myself. I paid several larger boys to beat up any boy who laughed at me. This worked wonderfully, and I always had more than enough money to pay for my protection. One boy, who lived close to us, was very good at this. He carried a knife and would actually stab other boys in the buttocks at my request. I paid him handsomely.

One might think, of course, that the upbringing described by Hans would be a custom-made background for the development of a predominantly homosexual orientation, and that the tormenting boys, so feared in his early childhood, would later become the sought-after objects of desire. *Why stab boys in the buttocks?* The answer is self-evident: that which you wish to touch, but which is denied to you, you punish. Hence the imagery common in a certain sort of erotic literature of boys bending over to be spanked.

But such conclusions would be quite wrong in relation to Hans: he liked girls, and found them sexually attractive, as Irmgard was to find out. That is why she stopped bathing him at eighteen. (Irmgard, by contrast, liked boys, whom she could pamper; when Hans became eighteen he ceased to be a boy and became a man, and therefore a threat.)

One could hardly describe this background as normal, and it was not surprising that when Hans began to go on dates with girls a certain pathology appeared. Once again, in confirmation of the point I made earlier on, dating proved to be the catalyst of distress.

Hans: I started to take girls out when I was seventeen. Irmgard discouraged it — she was fearfully jealous I think — but I took no notice of her. She said that girls were interested in only one thing. I said that I thought that was what girls said about boys, but she just said *Tutsch! Tutsch!* which is what she always said when she disagreed with anything one said. It was impossible to argue with her.

I no longer let her choose my clothes for me, but what I wore was still very important to me and I took a lot of trouble with my outfits. I used to like light blues, as these matched my colouring generally. I also liked russet browns and pale greens.

I spent a lot of time on my grooming. I had seventeen different brushes, and eight combs. I also had special lotions, which I used on different days. Monday was sandalwood. Tuesday was Bay Rum. And so on.

Self: Very ritualistic. Why did you spend so much time and energy on all this?

Hans: Because I wanted to look my best, of course — particularly when I took a girl out. They liked it too. They thought I was very smart, and they liked the way I smelled. No other boy smelled like that, they said.

We used to go to coffee bars and sit there for hours. I would sit near the window, if possible, so that I could see my reflection. Sometimes this irritated a girl, who would say something like: "I don't know why you bother to go out with me if all you're going to do is look at your reflection in the window." I would laugh at this sort of thing. "Suit yourself, honey," I would say. "You suit yourself. Lots of pebbles on the beach for Hansi!"

Had Hans said nothing more, the diagnosis would nevertheless have been confirmed beyond doubt. The narcissistic personality — an extremely difficult, unhappy condition for all concerned. Hans was in love with himself and would find no happiness until he had resolved that unsatisfactory relationship — a relationship which, by its very nature, was incapable of resolution! The implications, moreover, would reach further. Narcissus may be forever trapped in his own unhappiness, but he causes a great deal more unhappiness for others. He will search and search, and never find what he is looking for, because the person he is looking for is himself. And the problem with looking for oneself, is that the search is inherently impossible, because one can never see oneself from outside. Only the mirror is any help in that way, and Narcissus knows that the mirror is the cheapest of tricks. Poor Hans; but then:

Hans: I used to go out on five or six dates a week. Often I went with different girls in the same week, and that required planning — not to say cunning. I had to be careful that I would not go to the same coffee bar twice in succession, in case the girl I had been with the previous day would come looking for me there. They couldn't keep away from me. Yes, I did feel unhappy about it, but I couldn't really stop myself. It was as if I was looking for somebody — somebody who wasn't anywhere in Melbourne, or even Australia!

I suppose that some of the girls had reason to be annoyed with me. One, in particular, seemed to have it in for me more than the others . . .

It is not unusual to find that the narcissistic

personality gives rise in others to feelings of hostility. Some people resent being used for the self-gratification of the narcissist, and will try to do something about it. Often it's a gesture of desperation, though, which may have quite unexpected results . . .

Hans: This girl, *this real bitch,* called me up and told me that there was somebody who was very keen to meet me. But this person was shy and couldn't bring herself to ask me out. If I went round to her place, then, I would not be disappointed.

Who could resist an invitation like that? I certainly couldn't, and so I agreed to go that Saturday evening to an address which she gave me. I would be expected, she said — her friend couldn't wait.

I rang the door bell and it was opened — by myself. It was as if I was looking into a mirror. This fellow was exactly like me, exactly. He was my double.

We looked at one another for a while, our mouths open. Then he said: "They said it was a girl coming. I didn't expect you . . ." And I, of course, could have said the same thing, but I was completely at a loss for words. We were the victims of a cruel joke. This girl must have thought that I fancied myself.

Self: You must have been very happy, though, to see yourself standing there.

Hans: A bit, I suppose. But I still felt humiliated at what I saw as an insult. And I was worried, too, about this person who looked like me.

Self: You were worried because he looked like you, but wasn't you. So he was a rival.

Hans: If you say so. Anyway, I went away feeling pretty angry. And I still feel angry, which is why I've come to see you. Can you do something to help me?

Self: No. Nothing.

There is a postscript to the story of Large Hans. A few weeks ago I received a letter from him in which he said that he had made an extraordinary discovery. He had just been informed by his parents that they had been keeping something from him — that he had a twin brother who had died at birth. Hans knew now that he had found him, on that ill-fated meeting. Yet even this knowledge did not make him happy.

"I'm not looking for my brother," he wrote. "The last thing I want to find is a brother."

Now everything was clear. I had been quite ready to blame Irmgard for the development of Hans' narcissism, but that was probably only part of the story. Hans knew that there was another him — he had met him in the

180

womb and then he had lost him. And he had seen, in the womb, that his brother was his double. When, on growing up, he found that his brother simply wasn't there, then he knew, intuitively, that there was something missing — *and that something looked exactly like himself.* The ground was prepared for the narcissistic personality; Irmgard, her tin tub, her songs, and her Kaiser Franzi outfit merely cast the die that was already prepared.

I thought for some time that there was little that I could do for Hans, but suddenly I thought of advice which might just help. I invited him back to see me, and gave him my recommendation.

"Stop looking in vain for satisfaction in other people," I said. "Stop dating girls. Date yourself!"

He looked at me suspiciously.

"You mean I should go out . . . just by myself? Is that what you mean?"

"Yes," I said. "That's exactly what I mean. You'll be much happier — I'm sure of it."

He appeared to think for a moment.

"So I should go out and just . . . just dance by myself — that sort of thing?"

"Yes," I said. "You'll enjoy that. Also, take yourself out to dinner. Take yourself to the cinema. You're the person you really like, you know. Just accept that."

He smiled, clearly pleased at the suggestion.

"Perhaps you're right," he said. "Maybe

I've been wasting my time on all these dates with others."

"Of course you have. You're just right for yourself, Hans. I can assure you of that."

"And it'll be cheaper," he said. "Think of the money I'll save!"

"Yes," I said. "Fifty per cent."

His brow darkened. "But what about sex?" he said. "What about . . ."

I was prepared for this. "Who do you really want to find in your bed when you wake up in the morning, Hans? Whose head on your pillow? Answer me truthfully."

Hans smiled. "I suppose it's me. Yes, me. My own head."

"Well there you are," I said, adding: "You're happier now, Hans, aren't you?"

He smiled.

"A whole lot," he said.

CALWARRA

They did not live in Calwarra — which everybody simply called "town" — but about five or six miles out of it, along one of those dusty, half-paved roads that seemed to go on forever but led finally into the mallee scrub, to nowhere really. Their turning, marked only by a rickety signpost, was immediately after the grain siding, which was their landmark.

"First on the left, after the silos" — it was an easy, fool-proof way of directing visitors, who were rare anyway.

As a small child, she had played in their shadows, and had always thought of them as their silos, but of course they belonged to the town. It was here that the grain from all the surrounding farms was brought and loaded into the trains that would haul it off to port for shipment. For a few weeks of the year they were the centre of activity, as the harvest was brought in; for the rest of the year they stood deserted. Even then, though, the silos were the proof of the town's importance — its economic rationale. This is what explained Calwarra, what entitled it to exist in a country where a place could not be allowed to survive merely because it had always been there.

She lived alone with her father, who was sixty three now and ready to retire, if he could. Her mother had died shortly after her twelfth birthday, taken from them after an illness that had been brutally short. Afterwards, her father had retreated within himself, burying himself in his work on the land. Female relatives had offered to take her, and one aunt had even arrived at the farm and unwittingly pled her case within her niece's earshot.

"You can't look after a girl, Jack," she had said. "Girls aren't like boys. They need other women. They need somebody who can advise them on things. A father can't — he just can't — no matter how well-intentioned."

She had heard her father fight back.

"She's my child. This is her home. Damn it — a father's got a right to his own child, hasn't he? Have they done away with that now, have they? Have they?"

The aunt had changed tack. "She'll never forgive you if you keep her cooped up here. You're spoiling her chances. If she came to me down in Ballarat, then she'd grow up knowing how to get along, to make friends, to run a house. Things like that."

He had been silent for a moment. Then: "She can run this house. She'll get all the experience she needs — right here, where she belongs."

"But it's no life for a girl, Jack — see reason."

He had paused again before coming up with the reply that ended the discussion.

"All right," he said. "You ask her. You ask her whether she wants to stay here, where her home is — or go off to Ballarat with you. You ask her. They say we must consult children nowadays, don't they? All right. If she says she'll go with you, then you can take her. If she says she wants to stay, then she stays."

Her heart gave a leap. Of course she would say no: let them ask her, just let them ask her. Then they'd find out. But the aunt, realising, as did her brother, that children rarely choose to leave the familiar, knew that there was no point in posing the question. And so she snorted her resignation, muttering dire warnings as to what happened to girls who stayed on farms and never had the chance of a proper education. Then they moved to some other topic — some discussion about a disputed inheritance and the perfidy of a distant relative — and she lost interest, sitting alone in her room, the door still ajar, her quiet sobs for her mother unheard by the adults in the living room.

To the secret disappointment of his sisters, he managed well. Thwarted in their plans, only one of them ever complimented him, and grudgingly at that.

"She's turning out well, Jack," she had

said, when they met at a family wedding. "It can't have been easy for you."

But he had, in reality, found it easier than he had thought. He drove her into town, to school, each morning, and was never late in picking her up in the afternoon, whatever was happening on the farm. He bought her clothes himself, leaving the choice up to her, and she was always well turned out. He had waited grimly for the teenage rebellion, for arguments over staying out late, about accepting lifts back after parties from boys who had just passed their driving tests; but none of this came. Her friends — or such of them as he met — seemed pleasant and well-mannered. They were the children of other farmers, or of people in the town, and there were no surprises there. They had parties, of course, but on these occasions she was able to stay in town with friends, and she was always back on time, when she said she would be back. With a pang, he realised one day that under his nose, almost unnoticed, she had grown into her mother — a quiet, uncomplaining person, who could do everything and who took life in her stride.

The thought filled him with a curious pride. It would have been different, of course, if his wife had lived. She would have been able to give her so much more, but at least he had kept faith with her. In those last few, cruelly accelerated days in the hospital, they had been unable to talk although she knew exactly what was happening. All she had said about it was: "Look after her well, Jack"; and he had nodded, blinded by tears, unable to say anything himself.

At school, where the standards were low and the teachers for the most part mediocre and complacent, she did passably well. She was particularly good at art, and was encouraged by the art teacher, who unlike her colleagues had imagination, to think of going on to art school.

"You could get in," she said. "You could get a place in Melbourne, maybe even Sydney. And then afterwards, if all went well, maybe you could go on somewhere else. You could go overseas. The Slade. Paris. Somewhere like that. Imagine."

The girl's eyes shone; but she doubted that she would ever make it. She was a farm girl, raised out in the middle of nowhere, where you contended with ants, and foot rot in the sheep, and things like that. You couldn't just get on a bus and be transported to Paris, or even to Melbourne. Who would pay for it? Who would pay the fares? There was hardly any money as it was, and there would never be enough for something like that.

"Look," said the teacher. "I'm not just saying this. You could be an artist. It's a question of having the eye for it. And you've got it, you really have."

"Thank you." She was unused to compliments, and was unsure how to respond.

"Have you spoken to your father about it?" she pressed. "Have you discussed your future with him? What does he think you should do?"

She looked at the floor. They had not talked about it. Nothing had been said.

"Why don't you talk to him? Why don't you ask him about going off to Melbourne? There's no harm in raising it with him."

The teacher knew, of course. She knew that Jack Cogdon was one of those lonely, rather pathetic cases, hanging on to a farm that he really wouldn't be able to keep going forever, depending on his daughter to cook for him and keep house. She had seen cases like that before. But this one was different — this girl had talent. Some of the others were ideally suited for that sort of life — this one should be spared it.

She mentioned it at supper one night, after she had placed the plate of oxtail stew and vegetables before him, and taken her place on the other side of the table.

"I've got to think about what I'm going to do when I finish school," she said. "I've only got two more months."

He was taken aback, but he smiled at her weakly.

"It doesn't seem like that," he said. "Time flies."

She was silent for a moment, then: "Miss

Williams — you know her, don't you? — she thinks I should try for art school. Melbourne, maybe."

He dug his fork into his stew, avoiding meeting her gaze.

"Why not?" he said. "You do what you want to do. It's your life."

That was all he said, but she knew that he was unsettled. For the rest of the meal, he seemed anxious, although he tried to convey an impression of normality, raising small, unimportant subjects and moving quickly, inconsequentially from one to another. She knew, of course, what he was feeling. If she left, then he could never retire. He would work the farm until he was no longer capable of it, and then it would be sold. He would move to town, to one of those small houses that were filled with retired farmers who did nothing all day and hankered after their lost farms. What he wanted, of course, was for her to marry a farmer's son, who would take over from him; a farm boy, a boy who knew how to handle a place like this; somebody, in fact, like the youngest Page boy, who would never have the chance of his own place, with two older brothers ahead of him. By all accounts, he was a farmer through and through.

He said something to the father, over a beer in the Masonic Bar, where they occasionally met.

"I'll have to give up one of these days, I suppose. But I'm not as lucky as you, Ted. With your sons."

The other man smiled. "They can be tough little bastards to handle sometimes. You've had it easy, Jack." He paused, awkwardly. This was the unspoken tragedy among farmers — no son.

"Your youngest boy, though. You need to get him fixed up somehow. What's he going to do?"

The other man shook his head. "He's under my feet at the moment. He's been away working at Harrison's place, but they couldn't keep him on. There's plenty he could do, of course. He's a good mechanic. He can fix things. He could get taken on at some garage — serve his time . . ."

"But he's a farmer — bone deep."

"That's right."

For a few moments neither said anything. Then Jack looked up from his glass of beer.

"He might get on with my Alice. They might hit it off." He laughed. "Kids don't always see things the way we do, but why not . . ."

The other man smiled.

"They could do worse, couldn't they? He could get mixed up with some flighty piece of work who'd lead him a merry dance. She could find somebody, well, somebody who . . ."

"Your boy seems fine to me. I wouldn't have to get my shotgun out." He paused.

"Couldn't you drop the idea in there some-where?"

The other man looked dubious.

"You don't do that these days. Not in 1961."

Jack put down his glass. "Send him round to me to work. I'll take him on for a few months. I've got a lot of maintenance that needs doing. You said he could handle that."

"He could."

She wrote off to Melbourne, and they asked her to send them a portfolio of her work. This alarmed her, as she had kept very little, and had not really thought that anybody would ask to see her drawings.

"That doesn't matter," said the art teacher. "Do something for them specially. Send that. A portfolio doesn't mean a great heap of drawings. They just want to see what you can do."

So she did several pen and ink drawings — of the farmstead, of the silos, of still life, of one of her friends, and sent them off. She did not tell her father that she was applying; the discussion they had had was left curiously in the air, and she could not bring herself to raise the matter again.

Then she waited. The drawings had been posted from the school, and it was there that the reply would be received. Several weeks passed, and she imagined her drawings in

Melbourne, in a pile from all over the country, completely lost. But at last they wrote back and said they liked her work, but that they thought perhaps that it needed time to mature. They were pressed for places that year anyway, but they would take her, conditionally, for the following year, if she got the marks they wanted in her examinations.

"This means that you're in," said the art teacher. "You've got it, if you want. This business of waiting a year is probably quite a good idea. You can have a year out after school. A lot of people do it nowadays."

She took the letter home, buried between the pages of a text book, but could not bring herself to show it to her father. She extracted it, read it through again, and put it in her drawer, her private drawer where she kept her diary and her photographs. She would wait for the moment when she could discuss it with him — but it was a busy time at school, with the final examinations, and then the leaving dance. Somehow the time did not seem right, and her father, anyway, said nothing about what would happen after school came to an end.

She found herself making her own arrangements for the year. The bank had sent a circular to the school saying that they had two temporary vacancies which might suit people who had "not made up their minds yet". She went in to see the manager, who knew all about her, as everybody did of everybody else in the town, and who was quite happy to give her the job.

She told her father, and then she broke the news about the art college, which really could not be put off any further. He seemed unsurprised by what she said, almost as if he expected it, and told her that he would look into ways of finding the money for the fees.

"We've got time to think about all that," he said. "And you can save something from the bank. I'll run you in there each morning, same as usual."

Then he told her that the Page boy was coming to work on the farm for a few months.

"Do you remember him? The youngest Page boy?"

She frowned. "I think so. I get them mixed up, though. They were all a few years ahead of me at school."

"He's going to help me with some work on the barns and the tractors too. Apparently he's pretty good mechanically."

She nodded.

"What's he called?

"John," he said. "There's Bill and Michael, the two older ones. Then there's John."

He never had to tell him what to do. Without any help he stripped down the old harvester, which he had feared he might have to replace, and replaced all the engine rings. He scraped off rust, and dirt, and after a week or two had the engine running as sweetly as when it had been delivered, fifteen years ago. Then he started on the tractors, and he fixed them too, and painted the mudguards bright red, which was the colour he liked all his farm machinery to be.

She saw little of him at first, as she was away from the farm first thing in the morning, to be at the bank in time, and John was still living on his father's farm and driving over to work in a pick-up truck. Sometimes, though, he was still there when she arrived home at six, and she exchanged a few words with him.

She had noticed him, of course — in that way. He was tall, rather slender, and had that particular combination of dark hair and blue eyes that always caught her attention. She noted him down as good-looking, but did not think much more about him. He was just another boy from some farm; like all the other boys she had met at school, nothing special.

He was polite to her when he saw her, and stood up from his work and turned to talk to her, rubbing his dirty hands down the side of his work trousers. He spoke slowly, as if he was thinking carefully about what he was saying. He seemed to her to be rather old-fashioned, as if he were addressing an older woman, respectfully.

On the third weekend after he had started, her father asked him to join them for Sunday lunch. John arrived smartly dressed — she had seen him before only in his working clothes — and he had combed and slicked his hair down. He sat stiffly at the table, and smiled each time she spoke to him, as if on his best behaviour. Did he ever frown, she wondered, or did he inevitably smile?

After lunch, they drank tea on the verandah. Her father got up and went inside to make a telephone call, leaving the two of them alone.

"I hope that he's not working you too hard," she said. "You always look tired when I get home."

"I'm used to it," he said deliberately. "My old man has always worked us hard."

Then she looked at him, and he returned her stare, smiling.

"What about the bank?" he said. "Is that hard work?"

"Sometimes," she said. "Sometimes I don't have enough to do, and that's worse, in a way. I sit there and wait to be given something. The time goes pretty slowly."

He nodded. There was a silence. She looked out, over their sad attempt at a lawn and the bedraggled bed of cannas. She could make out the silos through the line of gum trees, and the dark line of the railway line snaking off into the brown. Then there was nothing, but the brown earth and a huge bowl of sky. There was nothing to draw here, she thought, nothing. You could start with an empty page and after a few lines everything would be recorded. Emptiness.

Suddenly he blurted out: "Would you like to go to a dance? There's one at the hall on Saturday."

She had not expected this, and did not think before she answered.

"Yes, I would." Then, seeing him relax, she added: "Thank you."

He spoke more quickly now, as they heard her father's footfall on the floorboards inside. "I'll pick you up at seven. On Saturday. Here."

"That's fine."

Her father rejoined them, lowering himself slowly into the decrepit wicker chair.

"I'm going over to Ballarat next Saturday," he said. "To play bowls. It's all arranged."

She nodded. "I'm going to go to a dance. John has just asked me. Is that all right?"

"Yes," he said, glancing at the young man, then quickly looking away again. "Fine."

She did not see him that week. He was doing some fencing work, and it kept him out on one of the far blocks. She thought of the dance, and wondered whether she should have accepted his invitation. Was he asking her out — on a date — or was this just a dance, to which everybody went, in a party or alone — it didn't matter very much.

What if it led to another invitation — to the cinema, for instance — which was less ambiguous? Should she go? Did she want to go? In one sense, she did. He was good-looking, and she liked the idea of going out with a boy whom her friends would notice. But she hardly knew him, she reflected. They had hardly spoken very much, and she real-ised that she knew nothing about him, other than his name, and that he could fix har-vesters and tractors.

He arrived earlier than he had said he would. Her father was not due back from bowls until much later, as they always had a drink after a competition. So she was alone in the house, and she called out to him from down the corridor, asking him to wait in the living room.

When she came in, he sprang up, his hands holding the sides of his jacket. He looked at her, and smiled, as always; he was pleased with the way she looked, she could tell; and she was flattered. He gestured towards the door, and they left, leaving a light burning in the sitting room for her father's return. In the cab of the pick-up it was cold, and there was a smell of dust. She hoped that he would drive slowly, so that dust would not come up from the road below and ruin her dress.

They travelled in silence. The road was

empty, as it always was at night, and the lights of the town in the distance were all that relieved the darkness. She fingered the strap of her handbag and thought: It is a date. This is it. This is going out with a boy.

The hall was lit up, and there were cars parked down each side of the street for the entire block. He nosed the pick-up into a space, and they went in, in to the light and the sound of the band tuning up. The women peeled off as they entered, and queued for the single, fly-specked mirror. She took a perfunctory glance, and went back to him, where he was waiting, awkwardly, at the entrance.

They found a table and sat down. He bought her a drink from the makeshift bar, a glass of cider, and poured himself a beer from a can. She glanced around her; she knew everybody, of course; there was nobody unexpected there. Even the band looked familiar; one of them, the drummer, worked in the bank. He caught her eye and winked. She smiled back.

The music started in earnest, and they danced. At the end of the first tune, she waited expectantly, but John did nothing. He just stood where he was, waiting for the music to start again. Then they resumed their dancing.

When they sat a number out, it was too loud to talk, and so they just sat at their table and looked around them. He mouthed something at her, but she could not make it out, and so she shrugged her shoulders. He bought her another cider, and she drank this, feeling thirsty from the dancing. Alcohol made her light-headed, quickly, and she felt the effect of the drink. It was not unpleasant.

At eleven o'clock, people began to drift away. John looked at his watch, and she nodded. In the cloakroom, while she retrieved her coat, she saw a girl sitting on the single chair provided, sobbing, her friend standing above her.

"He didn't mean it," the friend said. "He couldn't have meant it that way."

"He did," sobbed the other. "He did."

The friend looked up and caught her eye, sharing a moment of fellow feeling, as if to say: this is our lot. This is what we have to put up with. Men.

They drove back and parked the pick-up in front of the house. There was no light from inside, and the darkness was complete. They sat for a moment in an intimacy which she found not uncomfortable, but the words *what now?* went through her mind. The end of the date. What next?

He said: "I enjoyed the dance. Did you?"

"Yes. It was . . . It was great. I enjoyed it."

Then, suddenly he moved over towards her, and she felt his shoulder against her. He reached for her hand, and took it in his. She shivered, not knowing what to do.

This was what was next.

She felt him manoeuvre himself closer. He had moved her hand back, and it was lying against her chest. She felt his breath against her cheek, and then his lips. It's very strange, she thought. It's exciting. It's strange.

Now he was whispering to her: "Can we go inside? We could be quiet. We needn't wake up your old man."

She said, without thinking: "Yes. We can."

He said: "Don't turn on any lights. I'll take my shoes off."

They went into the living room, feeling their way round the furniture, and as they came to the couch, he reached for her and pulled her down with him. She let out a cry of surprise, but checked herself. Now they were on the couch, and he was smothering her with kisses, which she returned, putting her hands against the back of his neck. She felt his hands upon her, upon her shoulders, beneath her dress, and she wanted to stop him, but wanted him not to stop.

"Can we go to your room," he whispered. "It would be better there."

Again she wanted to say no, but did not, and they tiptoed down the corridor, past the shut door of her father's room. Then, still in the darkness, they lay down on the bed.

She came to, astonished, frightened. It was morning and he was still there, an arm across her shoulder, still asleep. She closed her eyes again, and then opened them, and he was still there, his chest rising and falling in sleep, his dark hair tousled. She shifted his arm from her shoulder and he stirred.

"Oh God!" he said, sitting up. "I didn't mean to stay."

He sprang to his feet, looking at his watch. She sat up too, thinking: Nothing really serious happened. We didn't make love. But she felt appalled by what had occurred, as if she had done something unforgivable.

"You can go out the back door," she said. "My father will probably be in the kitchen. Then you can go round to the front and get your . . ."

"He will have seen the pick-up," he said slowly. "He'll know I spent the night here."

She lay back on the bed, her hands over her eyes. And then she felt the bed sag as he sat down beside her.

"I'll speak to him," he said. "I'll go and speak to him right now."

"And tell him what? That we slept in?"

He shook his head. "I'll ask him if we can get engaged."

She kept her hands where they were.

"And what about me? Don't I . . ."

She thought of her father. How could she face him after this? How could she tell him — and be believed — that nothing had happened? He had said to her, embarrassed, on more than one occasion: One thing your mother believed in is keeping yourself for the man you're going to marry. Remember that.

He got up off the bed and she opened her eyes. She saw him cross to the door, hesitate a moment, and then turn the handle. Outside, the noise of the radio drifted from the kitchen. Her father was up. He would know.

The following Saturday they went to the cinema. He had bought her the ring, as he had said he would, and he slipped it on to her finger as they sat in the pick-up before leaving. Then he kissed her on the cheek, chastely, and started the engine.

They drove down the farm road, past the fence that he had spent all week repairing. It was almost dusk, and the last rays of the sun were soft fire on the fields. The road to Calwarra would be empty, as it always was, both on the way into town, and on the way home.

FAT DATE

He stood before the door, peering at the small brass plate above the bell. It was undoubtedly the right place, but he had expected something more than this somewhat anonymous sign. Still, that was an indication of good taste and discretion, which was exactly what one wanted from such a concern. It was a question of tact, really; the last thing one would want of people like this was flashiness or vulgarity.

He rang the bell and waited, examining a small notice that somebody had pasted to the wall: STAIR CLEANING. IF IT IS YOUR TURN, PLEASE REMEMBER TO MAKE SURE THAT YOU . . .

"Mr Macdonald?"

"Yes."

She smiled at him, not too enthusiastically, but just enough to set him at his ease.

"Do come in. We were expecting you."

He followed her along a small corridor to an office which overlooked the square. It was full summer, and there were trees outside the window, a shifting curtain of deep green. He took in the surroundings immediately. An office, but a personal office. There was a vase of flowers on the top of the filing cabinet, filled with a spray of carnations. Carnations: exactly right. You might have expected roses in a place like this, but that would have been too obvious.

"Please sit down."

She was behind her desk now, and she had opened a file in front of her.

"You haven't said very much about yourself on your form," she said.

He glanced at the piece of paper in her hand, recognising his rather spidery writing.

"I feel a little bit embarrassed writing about myself," he said. "You know how it is."

She nodded, gesturing with her right hand as if to say: of course we understand; everybody here is in the same boat.

"You see," she said, "we like to get things just right. It's really no good introducing people if they have radically different views of the world. Even a slight difference in musical taste may have a dramatic effect on the way in which people get on."

"Jack Spratt and his wife," he said, and then stopped. The words had come out without his thinking, but he realised immediately that the reference was ill-chosen. Jack Spratt could eat no fat, and his wife could eat no lean.

But she did not notice. "Yet in our case," she went on, "we have a good starting point. By catering specially for larger people, we manage to get round what some people see as a difficulty. If people have the same general conformation, then they start off with at least one thing in common."

He nodded. Yes. That was why he had chosen them. Perhaps he should not mince his words, at least when thinking. This was an agency for fat people. Dating for fatties! There, he had thought it! What would she have said if he had dared to say it? She would have written him off, no doubt, as a person with an attitude difficulty or a negative self-image problem.

"Now, I do have a few possible introductions for you," she went on, looking at him over her half-moon glasses. "There is one lady, in particular, an extremely charming person. I know her well. She and you share an interest in opera, I believe. She was married, some years ago, but sadly she is now divorced. It was really not her fault at all."

"It never is," he said. "It never is the stout person's fault."

A frown crossed her brow quickly, but then she smiled.

"There are awful injustices committed against more generously proportioned people," she agreed. "This was certainly so in this case."

They talked for a few more minutes. She served him coffee, poured from a tall white coffee percolator, and offered him a delicate chocolate biscuit. He took two and immediately apologised.

"I seem to have picked up two," he said.

She waved her hand. "Please. Think nothing of it. I have a weakness for chocolate too. Our shared little vice."

Now he stood outside the theatre, glancing nervously at his watch. She had said on the telephone that she might be a little late, but he had not expected to wait for fifteen minutes. If they were not careful, they would miss the beginning of the opera, and would not be admitted until the first interval. The possibility worried him. How would he entertain her in those awkward first few minutes. At least going to the opera gave them something to do.

But she had arrived now, leaping lithely out of a taxi in a shimmer of light blue voile.

"Edgar?"

He reached out and shook her hand.

"Nina?"

She held his hand for a few seconds longer than was necessary. "I knew it was you," she said, adding: "I'm so sorry for being late."

He thought for a moment. How did she know it was him? There could have been other men waiting — the street was by no means empty — but then he realised what it was. He was the only person in front of the theatre who could possibly have come from the introduction agency for fat people. He found the simple explanation unutterably depressing.

They went into the theatre. There was the usual opera crowd, some of whom he knew. He found this reassuring, and helpful. She noticed that people nodded to him and waved. I'm not a nobody, he thought. People know me about town.

"There's Fatty Macdonald," whispered one man to his wife. "Nice chap. Bit of an uphill battle, though."

"How do you know him?" the wife whispered back. "Work?"

"No, school. He was a year above me. We used to call him names and torment him too — you know how boys are. He had a terrible time, poor chap. Perhaps we could have him round for dinner some day and make up for it."

"I can't, I just can't. I've got so much to do. Look at next week, for example . . ."

They found no difficulty in making conversation during the interval. He was pleased to find that there was no awkwardness, as one might well expect on an occasion such as this. It all seemed wonderfully natural.

"I must confess I felt some trepidation," she said. "I've only had one or two introductions through them before. I'm not used to it."

He looked at her. "I've never been before. Ever."

"Well, you must have been feeling very nervous." She dug him playfully in the ribs. "Go on, confess!"

He laughed. "Well, I suppose I did. You never know how things are going to work out."

"Well, there you are," she said. "It really isn't awkward at all."

After the final curtain, they left by the side exit and walked briskly down the street to the Italian restaurant where he had booked a table. He explained to her that the place had been recommended by friends and that they specialised in after-theatre suppers.

"What a treat!" she said. "A wonderful way to spend a Tuesday evening!"

"Monday," he corrected.

They both laughed.

"Well, Tuesday as well, if you'd like . . ." He stopped. No. It was far too early to invite her out again. There should be a cooling-off period of a few days before he telephoned her and issued an invitation. That was what he had been told at the agency.

"Don't rush matters," he had been warned. "You've plenty of time to think things over. And women don't like being rushed either. Just wait until you've both had a certain amount of time to think about how you feel about one another."

In the restaurant, the proprietor led them to their table and drew her seat back with a flourish. She ordered a glass of sherry and he asked for a gin and tonic. Then they sat and looked at one another.

"I love Italy," she said. "I can't wait to go back there again. Florence. Siena. Verona."

"Rome," he said. "Venice. Bologna."

"Ah, Perugia. Urbino."

They were silent for a moment, while they both thought of something to say.

"I rented a house there once," he said. "I took it for two months and did nothing but sit on the terrace and read. I read and read."

"Ah."

"And then in the evenings I'd walk down to the piazza and watch everybody else watching everybody else."

"They're quite amazing," she said. "The Italians. They amaze me. They literally amaze me."

The silence returned.

"Do you like Italian food?" he asked. "I do."

"Oh, I do too," she said. "The herbs!"

"And olive oil," he added. "There is no substitute for olive oil, there really isn't."

"Edgar, I quite agree with you. There really is no getting round it. You have to use first pressing olive oil. You simply have to."

They ate well. She laughed as he struggled with his pasta; she had no trouble with it on her own fork.

"I just can't do this," he said. "I'm hopeless."

"I'll teach you one day," she said. "It is a bit of an art."

They raised their glasses to one another and sipped at the chilled Orvieto, sharp, straw-coloured. He imagined that he saw the colour of the wine go straight into her eyes, and she liked the idea.

"Perhaps it does," she said. "Anyway, what a nice thought!"

They drank more wine, and the proprietor brought a fresh bottle, tucked into its damp envelope of ice. Then, over coffee, he said:

"I must say that I was quite relieved to discover the agency. It really isn't easy if you're on the larger side. People seem not to want to know."

She nodded: "It's so unfair."

He warmed to his theme. "You know, thin people sometimes don't realise how cruel they're being. They laugh at us. They call us names."

"Yes," she said. "When I hear a child calling somebody Fatty, I say to him: Just you think how you'd like to be called that! Just you think! But most of the time they just can't imagine how other people feel."

He reached for the rest of the bottle of wine and filled their glasses.

"I was called names at school," he said.

"How awful," she said. "What were they?"

He glanced away.

"I forget now," he said. "It was a long time

ago. But if you think about it, you can't really blame children. They just take their cue from adults. Adults had it instilled in them when they were children, and so the vicious circle is perpetuated."

"And books contribute to the problem," she said. "Look at the way stout people are portrayed in fiction."

He nodded enthusiastically. "They describe us in an uncomplimentary way. They use words like *waddle* when they want to describe how a stout person walks. And films too. Look at the ridiculous things that happen to stout people in films. Absurd, slapstick things — people falling over, getting stuck and so on. As if life were like that!"

"You must have had an awful time," she said. "Imagine being called names at school."

He felt puzzled and rather annoyed by her reverting to his childhood. And he thought that she shouldn't have asked him what his nickname was. That was really rather intrusive.

"Why do you say I must have had a difficult time," he said, rather peevishly. "You must have had a tough time too."

"Me?" Her eyes opened wide with surprise.

"Yes. After all, you're just as stout as I am."

Her jaw dropped. "I beg your pardon," she said, her voice suddenly icy. "I certainly am not."

He put down his glass and stared at her, astonished.

"Oh yes you are. If you ask me, you're possibly even fatter."

"Oh! Oh!" She lifted her napkin to her mouth. "I don't know why you should suddenly decide to insult me. I really don't."

She rose to her feet, her voluminous blue dress flickering static in the semi-darkness of the restaurant.

"I'm very sorry it should end like this, but I have no alternative but to leave."

"It's your fault," he said. "You started it. And I am definitely not fatter than you. That's very obvious, if I may say so."

He got up to seek out the proprietor and pay the bill. The evening had suddenly become a complete disaster, and must be ended. But as he tried to get to his feet, the awful realisation hit him: he was stuck in his chair. He was completely wedged in.

He wiggled his hips, and then tried once more, but again with the same lack of result. He was stuck between the wooden arms of the chair and each movement only seemed to make the fit even tighter and less yielding.

She had noticed what had happened and was staring at him triumphantly from the other side of the table.

"There you are!" she said. "That proves it. I was right!"

He snorted angrily, and wriggled again. Now the proprietor had seen what was happening and had rushed to his side.

"I'm terribly sorry, sir," he said. "I shall get you free. Do not worry."

He bent down and began to tug at the wooden struts which held the top part of the chair together. He tugged sharply and there was a cracking sound. One of the struts came away.

"There we are," he said. "If I get a few more of these out, then you'll be able to release yourself. I am so sorry about this!"

She watched as the proprietor struggled. The real nature of the emergency had changed the situation somewhat, and she felt that she could not storm out now, as she had planned. She felt some sympathy for Edgar, even if he had insulted her. He did not deserve this embarrassment, this humiliation.

"I'm getting there," said the proprietor, crouched down, tugging at a piece of wood. "Perhaps this is a good advertisement for my food! Perhaps if everybody saw fat people like you coming in here and eating so well that they got stuck, then they'd know how good the food is!"

She drew in her breath sharply.

"How dare you!" she hissed. "How dare you talk about us like that."

Edgar was equally annoyed, and his heart gave a leap of pleasure when he saw her step forward and give the proprietor a sharp push. He was not expecting it, and he fell over, letting go of the strut of wood on which he had been tugging.

"Edgar," she said. "Get up and try to walk with that chair. We shouldn't spend a further second in this place."

He leant forward and pushed himself up, the chair still firmly wedged about him. Then bent double, he waddled out of the restaurant, with Nina close behind him.

The proprietor picked himself up off the floor and looked at the waiter.

"Ma, che cos'ho detto?" he said. *"Che cos' ho* fatto? *Che cos'e successo a quei grassoni?"* (What did I say, I ask you! What am I meant to have done? What's going on with these well-upholstered people?)

The waiter said nothing. He had not understood a vital part of the exchange and it seemed to him that the whole situation was utterly opaque.

Outside, it was a warm summer night. There were few people in the street to stare at him, and even those who were making their way home at that hour hardly noticed the sight of a large woman with an equally large, or possibly even larger man at her side, the man half-seated in a chair in which he appeared to be stuck.

"Sit down," she said. "Sit down on the chair. You'll be more comfortable. A taxi is bound to go past soon."

So he sat down, relieved to get the weight of the chair off him.

He looked up at her.

"I'm terribly sorry I was inadvertently rude in there. I really wasn't thinking."

She smiled. "And I'm sorry too. It was thoughtless of me. I hope you'll forget all about it."

"Of course," he said.

Then they waited in silence. Somewhere, in a flat in the narrow tenemental street, a record was being played; a fine tenor voice.

"Listen," she said. "Just listen!"

"How wonderful," he said. "How wonderful."

Then he patted his knee. "Why don't you sit down," he said. "We can sit here listening to that gorgeous sound until a taxi comes."

She smiled at him. Why not? It had been a fine romantic evening, apart from the one incident. She liked him. Perhaps they could face the indignities of the world together. Why not?

She adjusted her dress and lowered herself gently onto his knee.

Then the chair legs broke.

MATERNAL INFLUENCE

They still called her the Mayoress, although it had been years since she had held that office. It was just that she fitted the role so perfectly, and nobody, much to the chagrin of subsequent incumbents, had been able to live up to her. It gave her considerable pleasure to know that she was still referred to in this way, and in fact on several occasions she found herself on the point of using her old title and checked herself just in time.

Her husband had been the Mayor, although everybody knew that she made all the decisions for him. He was an extraordinarily mild man, who made no political enemies, and had therefore been the only candidate acceptable to all factions on a faction-riven town council. After his election, the councillors found that they had really got her, and it was too late by then.

Over the years of his first term, they became at first accustomed to, and then proud of her. She was magnificent, they felt, a galleon in full sail, carrying all before her on her bow wave; she was a civic treasure, in a sense, just like the Chain of Office and the Bank of South Australia Gold Cup (Best Cow).

Then the Mayor died. The District Auditor found him at his desk, slumped over a girlie magazine, mouth agape, his pale skin cold to the touch. The Auditor had quickly pushed him back in his seat and taken the magazine off the desk. Then he had put in its place a copy of the local water board estimates and pushed the slack body back over that. Only when he was satisfied as to the dignity of the death, did he rush out of the room and call for help.

He told only the doctor of what he had found on the Mayor's desk and he felt scandalised when the doctor laughed.

"Shock," he said. "Sexual excitement. It kills people, you know. His middle-aged heart couldn't take it. Finished him off."

"You're very callous, doctor. The Mayor was a good man, a family man."

The doctor snorted. "Don't be misled. I've seen things in my calling that would make your hair curl. Family men too. Just don't get me started on that."

The Mayoress bore her loss with dignity. She was happier, curiously enough, with the Mayor out of the way, although she had been fond of him in a comfortable sort of way. She still had her son, George, who was twenty seven and still living at home, and she had all her civic interests to keep her busy. The Mayor had been the proprietor of a large outfitters, which George was quite capable of running effectively, and the Mayoress had been left well provided for. A comfortable widowhood lay ahead; a time of fulfilment, she thought.

The Mayoress was fiercely proud of George, on whom she doted. She arose early every morning to prepare his breakfast — three pieces of toast, freshly squeezed orange juice, and poached eggs. Then she laid out his clothes on the table outside his bedroom door — suit, shirt (neatly ironed), socks, pants, braces, tie, shoes — everything.

By the time George came downstairs, the Mayoress would be at the table, ready to engage him in conversation. They would discuss the events of the forthcoming day, including the important question of what George would like for his lunch and his dinner, and what he proposed to do at the shop. Then, when George had finished his coffee, the Mayoress would run him to the shop in her car and drop him outside. She had always done this, although George had often indicated that he would prefer to drive himself.

"Nonsense," she said. "It's better for you to conserve your strength for the day's business. If I drive you, you arrive refreshed."

"But, mother, I really wouldn't mind driving. It's far easier . . ."

She silenced him with a glance. She had always found it easy to silence people by looking at them; it was something to do with her eyebrows and the way they arched. George could not argue. He was frightened of his mother, who had terrorised him — politely — since early boyhood. He had never once had an argument with her that had ended any way other than by his being cowed by the eyebrows. It was hopeless to try to change things now.

George was dissatisfied, but not overtly. If he stopped to analyse his feelings, what rankled was the frustration at not being able to stand up to her and to make his own decisions. She treated him like a boy, he thought, and yet it was so easy to remain a boy. It was his fault, he felt; he should be stronger. He should have the courage to live his own life.

He felt vaguely embarrassed about still living at home. Most of his contemporaries had set up by themselves in places of their own, had married, and some of them were fathers now. He was the only one left at home, and in a small town everybody would know that. He had once heard that somebody had referred to him as a Mummy's boy and the insult had cut deep. A Mummy's boy! Him!

He had once raised the question of moving out, but he had been silenced.

"What? Why do you want to do that? Is there anything wrong with your own home?"

He took a deep breath. "No, mother. It's very comfortable here. I know that."

"Well then, why move, may I ask?"

"It's just that . . . well, I feel it might be rather fun to have my own place. You know?"

She had smiled at him, as if trying to humour a recalcitrant schoolchild.

"Your own place? Your own place, George? Isn't this *your own place,* as you call it? Does this belong to anybody else? Aren't the deeds in your name as well as mine, as Daddy said in his will? What more do you want?"

"Daddy was thinking of tax problems. That's why it's in my name too. Mr Quinlan spelled all that out. It's for when you die."

She had narrowed her eyes, just a little, but he noticed.

"Die, George? Am I about to die then?"

"Of course not, mother, but look at Daddy. He died."

"I am only too well aware of that," she said, her voice chilling. "Your Daddy died of overwork. He spent all his time working hard to make money for you and me to live in this house afterwards. The best house in town, by far. And now you're talking about abandoning it."

"I wasn't talking about abandoning it, mother. I was just wondering whether it might not be a good idea to have my own place. I'd come back here at weekends."

"But, George, why leave a perfectly good home, where you've got everything you could possibly need, just to move out into some wretched, poky little place down by Griffiths Street or wherever. What's the point? You could be Mayor one day, you know."

He did not conceal his astonishment. "Mayor?" And whispered under his breath: *Bum*.

"Yes, George. Mayor. Somebody said to me the other day that you would be ideal, just like Daddy. And this house will help you. You need to have something behind you to be Mayor in a town like this."

"I don't want to be Mayor, mother. Being Mayor was fine for Daddy. I'm different . . ."

But by then he saw the eyebrows beginning to rise, and the subject had been dropped. For a few moments there was silence, and then she announced: "There's a new consignment of velvet at Baxters. They're letting me have first look over it and I thought I'd make new curtains for your bedroom. What colour would you like? Same as usual?"

He had mumbled something noncommittal and had left the room disconsolately. She's horrid, he thought. She's a big fat bitch. She's a bag. She's a bloody battle-axe. Bum. She's a spider.

This made him feel much better, and he called his dog, to take him for a walk round the block. Cecil, who was a heavily-built Alsatian, jumped up in excitement and licked enthusiastically as the metal choke chain was fitted around his neck. Then together they set off, bachelor and dog, and while Cecil panted and strained at the leash George thought of what he would do. I'm going to get a girlfriend, he thought. I'm going to go out with somebody. I'm going to find a girl with big breasts and blonde hair. That'll show her. Then I'm going to buy my own place — she can't stop me — and I'm going to move out. I'll make my own breakfast and iron my own shirts. I don't care. I don't care!

He looked down at Cecil, his friend.

"Do you remember Daddy, Cecil? Do you remember that other man who used to take you for walks? Do you?"

The dog looked back at his owner and tugged harder at the leash.

"Daddy was kind to you, Cecil. He gave you bones. Poor Daddy. He was a nice chap, our Daddy. You try to remember him. I know it's hard if you're a dog, but you just try."

He worked out a strategy over the next few days. First of all there was a telephone call to his friend Ed. He had been at school with Ed, and although they had little in common, Ed had proved a loyal friend. He had helped Ed out on one or two occasions when he had got into financial difficulties, and Ed had always been grateful. Ed spent far too much on cars, and he had lost one or two jobs. He survived, though, and seemed to relish his precarious existence.

Ed agreed to meet him in the bar at the Central Hotel after work that Wednesday.

"I want your help, Ed," he began. "It's a tricky thing."

"You tell me, mate. I owe you a few."

"It's about a girl, Ed."

Ed had smiled. "Trouble, George? Well, you old dog! You got some dame up the spout? Well, well! What would the Mayoress — beg pardon, George — what would the old lady say about that? Not too pleased, hey?"

He shook his head. This was not proving easy.

"Ed, the truth of the matter is I don't really know many girls and I was wondering whether you could help me out. You know lots. Maybe you could introduce me to some suitable ones, then I could . . . well maybe I could choose, sort of."

Ed lowered his beer glass and stared at his friend.

"I'm not so sure it works like that, mate. You know, women get ideas, sometimes. They got their own notions. They like some guy enough to tear his trousers off, you know. That's fine. That's just as it should be. Then sometimes, no deal. Nothing doing."

George looked at Ed. "Oh, I see."

"But not to worry," Ed went on, brightening. "I know plenty of girls who are real desperate and who would really like a nice, homely — beg pardon — bloke like you. Some of them would be pretty pleased to have somebody respectable — solid — around the place. No, the more I think of it, George, the more I think you'd be a wow with the girls, or with a certain type of girl. What do you want me to do?"

George cleared his throat. The conversation was making him feel hot around his neck. It was awkward to have to talk to Ed like this, even if he knew that the other man was not the sort to find this sort of thing embarrassing.

"Could you have some sort of party, Ed? Down at your place. Then I could come and meet some of the girls you know. And who knows? There might be one who's suitable. Who knows?"

Ed raised his glass in a mock toast.

"No problems, mate! No problems! Next Friday suit you? Fine! I've got some real goers on the books, I'm telling you. They'll raise your temperature bloody quick, George! You'll see, mate! You'll see!"

He prepared carefully for Ed's party. He informed the Mayoress that he was going out, that he had to go and see Ed about

224

something and that he would probably stay and talk to Ed for a while.

"Don't expect me back till quite late," he said casually. "In fact, it'll probably be best for you to turn in. I'll just let myself in."

She looked at him. "That late? My goodness, you must have a lot to talk to Ed about. He's that rather . . . rather dirty one isn't he?"

"Ed's not dirty," he said quietly, and under his breath: *Bum! Bum!*

"Of course not," she said. "I didn't really mean that he's still dirty. It's just that when he was a boy he used to come and play here and he always seemed a bit dirty to me then. Boys so often are. I'm sure he's not dirty any more. He used to be, though. Very dirty."

He came home early on Friday evening to prepare. He was pleased to find that she was out, which meant that he did not have to sneak out the back way, as he had planned. Had she seen him in his best clothes, she would have suspected something.

He showered, slapped cologne on his cheeks, and then put on the new trousers and shirt which he had taken out of stock that day. Then he went into the kitchen to feed Cecil.

"I'm off to a party, Cecil. You're staying here. Be a good dog and I'll bring you something back from the party. If your Uncle Ed gives us bones, that is. Hah hah! No chance, Cecil. Bad luck."

The Alsatian looked at him, wagged his tail, and then dozed off again. George turned off the kitchen light, locked the front door behind him, and drove off slowly to Ed's house on the other side of town. He felt overwhelmingly excited. This was the beginning of a whole new chapter, a whole new life. It was the end of boyhood, definitely, definitely. Ten years too bloody late! *Bum!*

Ed was at the door, having just admitted a guest.

"George! There you are. Party's just beginning. Going well too, know what I mean!"

George followed his host into the living room. There were ten people already there, sitting on sofas and standing by the tables. There was music on the record player.

"I'll introduce you," said Ed. "Guys, this is George. George — Mike, Terry-Anne, Marge, Tom, Darlene, Beth, What's-his-name, Mac, Linda and that's Meryl in the kitchen, just coming out."

George looked at Meryl, who smiled at him. She was carrying a large tray of pizza, which had been cut into small squares. She pointed with her free hand to the tray and brought it across to offer him a piece.

"Straight from the oven, George. Like a piece?"

He selected a slice and took a small bite. The cheese was still molten, and he burnt his tongue slightly, but he did not show his discomfort.

"Fabulous," he said. "Did you make it?"

Meryl laid the tray down on a table and helped herself to a small segment.

"Yes. I love making pizzas. I love making Italian food. I just love it."

"I can't really cook," said George. "I wish I could."

"So who cooks for you?" asked Meryl. "Your girlfriend?"

George looked down at his shoes, his new suede shoes with the fancy toe-caps. They had been the best line in the shop by far.

"My mother, actually."

Meryl smiled. "That's lucky. I bet she's a good cook."

George thought of the shepherd's pies and the casseroles.

"She isn't," he said. "She can't cook to save her life."

"Oh," said Meryl, licking the tips of her fingers. "Well I'm sure she's good at other things."

"No," said George. "She isn't. She can order people about, that's all."

Meryl laughed uneasily. "Mothers are like that. Mine tries to order me about, but I don't take any notice."

He said nothing. He was looking at her carefully now, at her blonde hair, which was piled up, bouffant-style, and at her blouse (discreetly). Yes, she was just right. The Mayoress would *hate* her.

They sat down on a sofa and talked. Meryl seemed relaxed, and was happy to talk to him about anything that came into her mind. He told her about the shop, and about his plans for the new showroom. He told her about his trip to Adelaide. He told her about Cecil, and how the vet had pinned his leg when he had been run over by the dustcart.

"You wouldn't think it was broken in six places," he said. "Just looking at him today, you wouldn't think that."

She nodded. "Vets can work wonders," she said. "They're better than doctors — some of the time. A vet fixed my uncle up when he broke his leg in the outback. He hardly limps at all these days."

"The vet couldn't do anything about his halitosis, though," he said. "He said that he could try pulling all his teeth out, but if he did that he wouldn't be able to gnaw on his bones. That would be cruel."

"You could give him garlic pills," she said. "That might help. Put them in his dog-food."

Ed came round with another beer for George and a glass of rum and coke for Meryl.

"You two getting on fine?" he said, winking at George. "Lots to talk about?"

George laughed. "You've got some nice friends, Ed."

He thought that Meryl blushed when he said this, but she looked pleased.

"Damn right," said Ed. "Meryl here's a real sport, aren't you Mez?"

He reached down and pinched her on the cheek, and she brushed his hand away playfully.

"I'll leave you two, then," said Ed. "No need to take petrol to a fire, know what I mean!"

George thought the party was a great success, apart from the end, when Ed, who was by then fairly drunk, hit one of the other guests. He apologised immediately, and Mike, who had been hit, tried to smooth over the argument.

"Sorry, Ed, I didn't mean it. Just let's forget it, see."

"I'm sorry too," mumbled Ed. "I get carried away, you know. I don't know what came over me — beg pardon."

"No hard feelings," said Mike. "Let's forget it."

But the tone of the party had changed, and the other guests began to disperse. George offered to drive Meryl home, and she accepted his offer.

"I can't stand it when Ed gets drunk and hits people," she said. "I know he means no offence, but one of these days somebody's really going to hit him back, hard."

"Why does he do it?" George asked. "You'd think he'd learn."

"He can't help himself," said Meryl. "It's just his nature. Like some people are musical."

They were driving past the shop now, and George slowed down.

"There it is," he said. "It looks good, doesn't it."

"Yes," said Meryl. "You've got some high-class clothes in there. I've always said that."

"I'm going to open a new section for teenagers," said George. "I'll call it *The Young Idea*. We'll play disco music and have flashing lights. What do you think of that?"

Meryl was impressed. "That's a really good name," she said. "Original. They'll love it."

They drove on in silence. George was waiting for his moment, and now he judged that it had arrived.

"Would you like to go to the . . . the . . ." He began to stammer. "To . . . to . . ." *Bum!* he thought. Why do I have to bloody stammer just when I'm trying to ask her out?

"Yes," said Meryl. "I'd love to."

"To the cinema," he blurted out.

"Yes," said Meryl. "When?"

"Tomorrow?"

"Love to," she said. "You get really good ideas, George. Did you know that?"

At breakfast the next morning, the May-

230

oress looked reproachfully at her son.

"You must have been very late last night," she said, passing him his glass of orange juice. "Did you enjoy yourself?"

"Yes," he said, gazing intently at his toast. "I did."

"And how's our friend Ed?" she said. "Has he got a job these days?"

"Yes," he said. "He's working at Rileys. It's quite a good job."

She digested the information silently.

"Anybody else there?" she asked after a while. "Or was it just you?"

"A few others," he said. "Nobody you know."

She pursed her lips, but he did not notice, as he was now scrutinising the label of the marmalade jar.

"I'll be late back tonight as well," he said. "I've got work to do."

He shot a glance up; the eyebrows were raised, and he looked away again quickly. Then, before she could say anything more, he sprang to his feet, picking up his toast.

"It's late," he said. "Don't bother to drive me in today, mother. I want some exercise. I'll walk."

Her mouth dropped open as she searched for words.

"But . . . If it's late, then you shouldn't . . . You . . . I always take . . ."

But he had left the room and she was

alone with Cecil. The dog stared at her from the other side of the room, his watery eyes expressionless.

"Get out!" she said suddenly. "Get out, you smelly creature! Out!"

He collected Meryl from her shared flat and they drove into town. There were plenty of parking places outside the cinema and he parked in one of these. Then they went in, purchased a large barrel of popcorn from the refreshments counter, and entered the comfortable air-conditioned cocoon of the cinema.

There were advertisements to begin with, and the trailers of the forthcoming attractions.

"We should go and see that one," he said, naturally, without thinking, and she agreed.

"Good idea."

He felt a warm flush of satisfaction. They were going out together! She had accepted his second invitation! This might be their first date, but there were going to be more! He would propose to her in a few months' time — maybe even a bit earlier — and he was sure that she'd say yes. They could run the shop together. They could build a house over in that new development — *Executive Hills* — it would be bliss! They would take Cecil, of course, but leave her! Hah!

Then, just before the film was due to start,

a large figure eased itself into a seat directly in front of them.

"Typical," Meryl whispered. "Some old duck comes and sits right in front of you when the film's about to start."

George froze. It was impossible. It couldn't be! It was a nightmare. The Mayoress turned round, as if accidentally.

"Well, well!" she said. "Fancy seeing you here! I thought you were working."

She half-turned in her seat to look at Meryl.

"Aren't you going to introduce me, George?"

George could barely speak, but Meryl was looking at him, and so he made the introduction.

"This is my . . . my . . . my . . ."

"Mother," said the Mayoress. "Pleased to meet you. And you are . . . ?"

"Meryl."

"Look, I'll just come and sit beside you, Meryl. It'll save me getting a crick in my neck."

The Mayoress got to her feet and pushed past George to sit on the other side of Meryl.

"I do hope this film is good," said the Mayoress, her voice sickly sweet. "Do you like the cinema, Meryl?"

The lights dimmed.

"We'd better save our conversation for the

interval," said the Mayoress. "The film's starting now."

George said nothing in the interval. He looked straight ahead, trying to block out the sound of his mother's conversation with Meryl. Meryl did her best to deal with the Mayoress's questions, which came thick and fast, but it was clear that she was finding it a strain. From time to time she looked at George in mute appeal, but he could not help her.

At the end of the show, the Mayoress rose to her feet and suggested that they all go home for a cup of hot chocolate.

"George likes to go to bed early on a Saturday," she said. "We always go to early communion, don't we, George? And it's easier to get up if you're in bed early. George's Daddy always used to say that."

They walked out of the cinema, and at the front door, the Mayoress said: "You drive ahead. I'll see you at the house in a few minutes."

They got into the car. George reached forward and turned on the engine. Then he noisily reversed out of the parking place, swung the wheel round, and accelerated down the road.

"I'm sorry," he said. "I'm really sorry about that. I can't help my m . . . moth . . . mother. I can't . . ."

"Don't worry," said Meryl. "I thought she was quite nice really."

"She isn't," said George. "I hate her."

Meryl bit her lip. She had noticed the look of pain on his face, and now she saw that it had been replaced by an expression of determination. She saw him look in the driving mirror and she saw the headlights behind them. George pressed his foot down on the accelerator and the car lurched forward. The car shot ahead, and the lights behind them dimmed for a few moments. Then they were at a corner and George braked sharply and brought the car into a screeching turn.

They shot down the side-road. Behind them, the lights of the other car slowed down and then made the turn too. George looked behind them and speeded up again. There was another turning, and a turning after that, but still the lights followed them.

"Who is it?" she asked. "Who's following us?"

"Who do you think?" George muttered.

She did not answer. They had reached a roundabout, and he had taken the car up over the grassy verge and across the centre. They bumped down on the other side and he pulled off into a tree-protected stop just beyond. He turned off the engine and the lights and glanced into the mirror.

The other car was now travelling more slowly. It paused at the roundabout and then made a full circle, its lights sweeping out over the lawns of the houses on either side of the road. Then, more slowly, it began to move away along the route by which it had come.

"That's got rid of her," said George. "And good riddance."

She moved across the seat towards him. "It's nicer to be just by ourselves," she said. "Much nicer."

"That's how a date should be," said George, stroking her hair. "Just two people. No mother."

The next morning, George was down at breakfast early. By the time the Mayoress came downstairs, he had finished his toast and was drinking his second cup of coffee.

"What's that?" she asked, pointing to the suitcase that stood in the middle of the room.

"My suitcase, mother," he said, pouring more milk into his coffee cup. "That's what that is."

"Where are you going?" she asked. "It's Sunday, you know."

"I am well aware of that, mother," he said. "I'm moving out. I'm going to go and stay with my friend Ed for a few days while I look for my own place."

She glanced around her for a chair, and sat down heavily.

"Don't be ridiculous, George." She was struggling to keep her voice even. "There's no call to move out. You aren't cross about last night for some strange reason are you? Did I do something to upset you?"

He looked over towards her, but he did not dare meet the gaze. That would have been to look into the eyes of Medusa.

He rose to his feet. "My mind is made up," he said. "I'm going. Goodbye."

The Mayoress stood up.

"George," she said imperiously. "Look at me! I forbid it! Imagine what . . . Imagine what Daddy would think! Just think what Daddy's saying in Heaven right at this moment!"

But he had called Cecil over to his side and was preparing his leash. She took a few steps towards him, but he drew back and raised his voice:

"Don't come near me, mother. Just let me go."

"George!"

She advanced a step or two closer, but he had pulled Cecil round to face his mother and was pointing at her.

"Cecil," he said. "See her off! See her!"

Cecil looked up at his master, as if for confirmation of a manifestly illegal order.

"See her off, Cecil! See her!"

The Alsatian growled, and the Mayoress stood quite still.

"George! How dare you! How dare you! Tell that ridiculous dog to sit."

But Cecil was inching towards the Mayoress, his hackles raised, a low growl coming from his throat. She moved back slowly, and the dog pressed his advantage. Then his growl became louder, and he showed his teeth, old, yellow rotten teeth, but still fang-like in appearance.

The Mayoress was now close to the door that led back into the hall, and she suddenly turned and lurched through it, slamming it behind her.

"Good boy, Cecil," George said. "Now you come with me. We're going to Ed's. Remember Ed, Cecil? He won't mind your bad breath. He likes dogs like you."

They left the kitchen, George carrying his suitcase in one hand and holding Cecil's leash in the other. It was a wonderful morning outside — fresh and exhilarating. Ed was expecting him almost immediately, and then he was going over to Meryl's for lunch. She had said that she knew somebody who had a flat to let, which she thought might be big enough for two, and a dog. It was a marvellous prospect. Marvellous.

Cecil gave a bark.

"Good on you, Cecil," he said. "Woof bloody woof. That's the spirit!"

HEAVENLY DATE

Lunch was taken on the terrace, as it always was. She had cut several slices of white bread — the thick, crusty bread which Signora Sabatino baked — and she laid them out on a plate alongside ham, olives, and mozzarella. It was his favourite lunch — a meal that he said he could eat only in Italy. They would sit, father and daughter, shaded by the pergola, and look down the valley to the blue hills beyond. She liked to throw the olive stones over the parapet in the hope that they would root and make an olive grove one day; already there were saplings from previous years. He would watch her with amusement, sipping from the glass of wine which he always had with his lunch, while she drank mineral water from large bottles decorated with the certificates of chemical analysts. *Professore Eduardo Militello of the Istituto Idrobiologico of the University of Parma testifies to the contents of this bottle as follows: calcium . . .*

She loved the sound of the names. She loved the signatures and the elaborate, flowery language. What did a *professore idrobiologico* actually do? She imagined bubbling, sulphurous realms in the cool depths of an ancient university building.

"I inevitably want to fall asleep when I arrive here," he said, reaching out for a piece of bread. "Italy has that effect on me."

She smiled. "There's nothing wrong with doing nothing."

"I really should retire," he said. "This place could do with somebody living in it permanently. Not just for a few months each year, but all the time."

He put his glass down and lay back in his deckchair.

"What are your plans? Do you really want to stay out here until it's time to go to university? Are you sure about that?" His voice was lazy, but this concealed concern, anxiety.

She nodded. "I love it here," she said. "I always have. And you've just said that this place needs more attention."

He looked dubious. "But surely you could be doing something more with this year? Going somewhere else, for example — Australia, Canada. I've got plenty of contacts there. You could have an interesting time, you know that."

Then he added: "Life closes in afterwards. It really does."

"But I don't want to go anywhere else," she said. "I might never have another chance to spend a long time here. I can visit those other places later on."

"But what are you going to do all day?

There's nothing much to do here. You'll go mad with boredom."

"I won't. I'll read. I'll get the bus into Siena. I'll sign up for a music course there. I'll get the details."

"If you're sure . . ." He sounded doubtful. He did not want to begrudge her this freedom, but she was his only child, everything he had now.

"I'm sure."

The house had been built in the seventeenth century, or at least its heart dated back that far. Over the years there had been additions, which merged almost imperceptibly with the original building, but which resulted in an appealing architectural eccentricity. It was a house of surprises; of vast rooms, which turned corners; of corridors that led nowhere; of cupboards that became cellars. He had felt that even when he had bought the house — after interminable legal wrangles — he had not become its owner; that the house belonged to no one, or at least to no one who was alive.

They shared it with animals. There was a small colony of bats, which clung tenaciously to the brickwork of an outer wall and which squealed and dipped across the sky at dusk. There were several cats, who were the progeny of the half-feral cats who had been there when he had first inspected the place, and who were overfed by Signora Sabatino, the caretaker. There was a family of foxes who lived in an old shed that was propped up against a storeroom wall; and there were mice, of course, never seen, but heard, scurrying within ceilings and behind skirting boards.

He had bought the house to please his wife, who loved Tuscany. It would be a new beginning, he had thought, and for a while it had worked. It was rather like having a child again — something for which they were both responsible — but it had not lasted. She was bored with him, he knew, and she could not conceal her impatience. They had spent one last week there together, but the last days had been heavy — an ordeal of emptiness and forced politeness. And when they left, he knew that they would never be there again, that their marriage was over, and that she would go back to America, to take up her own life again. There were people there who cared for her. He had never been able to make much of them, and he had at last realised they simply weren't interested. They were incapable, he thought, of understanding anybody who was unfamiliar to them; who did not share their way of looking at things, their accent — their private culture — their particular preoccupations. He felt that they were mildly surprised, in a way, that other people — people outside America — actually existed.

At least Emma stayed with him. She had never been particularly close to her mother — who was bored with her too — and although she had expressed regret at her mother's departure, she had seemed largely unaffected by it. So now there were just the two of them, happy enough, in their way; a man in his fifties, a trader in obscure markets, with an office in the City of London, and all his agents, a man whose life did not mean very much in particular; and a girl of nineteen, expensively educated, rather on the dreamy side perhaps, but with an idea that something would happen to her, that life would start soon enough, and that it would be quite in accordance with the script she would write for it.

He hoped that she might change her mind after a week, and agree to come back with him, but she did not. He spoke to Signora Sabatino, who lived in a small house on the edge of his land. He knew that she was fond of Emma, and that she would protect her in the same fierce way in which she protected the property against intruders, and this made it easier. He would have refused — had a row even — if Emma had wanted to stay there entirely by herself.

As he had expected, Signora Sabatino was delighted that she would have company. He had difficulty following what she said, as his

Italian, unlike Emma's, was barely adequate, but her pleasure was clear.

"I will see that she writes to you," she said. "Every week, understand? She'll write a letter. You just see!"

He smiled. "Good," he said, making a mental note to pay her more. She lived rent free, in exchange for her duties, but he knew that she had little money. He could make the difference so easily, and he had long known that, but had never done anything about it. Now he felt shame that the gesture would come only when he really needed to rely on her. On the day before he was due to leave, they walked up to the Church of San Cosimo. It was a favourite spot for both of them — a tiny church, still in good order in spite of being long abandoned by priest and congregation. It clung to the edge of a hill, reached by a white dust track that led up to a straggle of vineyards. At the side door, which was locked, there was a slot in the stone with the legend — FOR CHARITY — carved above it in weathered lettering. They always pushed a coin through this slot, as a shared joke, which had became half-superstitious, and they had no idea where the coin ended up. There was no sound, no clink of metal, as the offering was swallowed up in the silent church.

He had read, to his surprise, that it was a criminal offence in Italy to destroy or abandon the currency. There had been trouble some years previously when, in a time of coin shortage, it had been discovered that the Japanese had been exporting Italy's small change to make the coins into buttons. National honour had been involved, and there had been threats to invoke the law. But he liked the idea that his clandestine giving was also an offence. It was as if, in a time of religious suppression, he had found a priest hole, with a priest still hiding inside.

That day, after sitting for a few minutes outside the church, they walked further up the track towards the vineyards. They occasionally saw people working here, pruning the vines or scratching at the soil beside the gnarled stems, but today there was nobody. They found a cart, though, an ancient vehicle with tyres of solid rubber, and with red wine stains across its board. She sat on the cart, and then lay on it, staring up at the sky.

"I wish you didn't have to go back," she said. "We could just live here, always. I could be one of those Jane Austen daughters who just stays at home and looks after her father."

"That would be very pleasant," he said. "Until you got bored and went off with some romantic Neapolitan."

"Then you could marry Signora Sabatino," she said. "I'm sure she'd accept you. You could help her with her chickens."

He laughed at the suggestion, for a moment imagining himself in the vast *letto matrimoniale* which he had glimpsed in the interior of Signora Sabatino's house, the one item of comfort so cherished in the peasant household. But the pain of their impending parting cut at him. He knew that this is how it would be from now on; she had become an adult, and his time with her would be as a visitor, in a life that revolved around others. It must be easier to let go, he thought, when you have something else in reserve.

For the first few days after his departure, it felt strange to her, to be in the house by herself, so utterly alone. She slept badly, frightened by the daytime silences of the house and by the noises it made at night. As the heat of the day died away, the roof creaked and shifted, as if trying to find rest, and at first these noises sounded like doors opening, or windows being forced. But she became accustomed to them, and she began to sleep less fitfully, going to bed early and waking late.

She was thrilled by the freedom. At school her life had been regimented, with only small islands of opportunity for independent choice. And there had been noise, everywhere; bells, feet in the corridors, the drone of others' radios, arguments. Now she could make her own decisions; get up when she wanted to; go down to the village for groceries when it suited her; go for a walk, or stay or read. The freedom felt almost tangible, a cloth that one might weave as one wished, into whatever pattern suggested itself.

She travelled into Siena on the fourth day. There was a bus that ran from the village and the journey took only an hour. She found it strange to be back in a town again, but she knew Siena well and always felt comfortable there. She sat for an hour or so drinking several cups of strong black coffee, watching people walking in the piazza. There were children with brightly coloured flags, in the colours of the *contrade*, women talking, pigeons fluttering up from the fountain or swooping out from the tower when the bells rang.

She made her way to the office of the university where arrangements were made for enrolment on courses. She was shown into a waiting room, where she sat on a bench beneath a picture of a man playing a lute, and then, after twenty minutes, was called into an office.

There was a man behind a desk, a man with a sallow complexion, dressed in the dapper light suit chosen by Italian bureaucrats during summer. He half rose to his feet, gesturing to a chair in front of his desk.

"You are interested in one of our courses?" He spoke softly, and she had some difficulty making out his question.

"Shall I speak in English?" he added quickly.

"There is no need."

He explained to her what they had to offer, and handed her several brochures. One of the courses, which lasted three months, seemed ideal — the history of Italian music from the fourteenth to the nineteenth centuries.

"Yes," he said. "You could do that. That would be a good course for you."

Then there was silence for a few moments, and he stared at her. She felt disconcerted by his gaze; by the wide, brown eyes, that seemed be searching for something. Then he spoke.

"It is so hot," he said. "I wish that I were away altogether. Down at the coast. Anywhere. Away from here. Wouldn't you like to be there too?"

She said nothing, but filled in the form which he had passed her. Then she handed it over, and he sighed.

"This is all in order," he said. "The music school will write to you to let you know their decision. But I'm sure that they will say yes. They always say yes."

He smiled weakly, as if to imply that he, a bureaucrat, understood the liberal ways of academics. Then, as she arose, he went quickly over to the door and opened it for her, standing too close to her as she passed by. She noticed his hand, the ring, and the tiny crow's feet about his eyes, and she wondered why they felt that they had to bother, these Italian men. What point were they making?

The course did not start for another month, which suited her. She could do some reading, she thought — she had bought some books in Siena — and tutor herself in music history before her classes began. She could go for long, aimless walks, and learn from Signora Sabatino how to bake bread; she could write letters. She would not be bored, she was sure of it.

It was quite clear that her presence in the house had transformed Signora Sabatino's days. Each morning the caretaker brought a basket of fruit and vegetables for her kitchen, and every two or three days there were eggs, fresh from the hens, dark yellow in their yolks, tasting of the dry countryside.

They spent hours talking to one another, and she found that as the days passed and the older woman got to know her better, she was prepared to reveal to her much about her life which she would not otherwise have learned. There was the story of the brother who had become a priest and then, to the shame of them all, had suffered some disgrace and had been sent off to a mission in Ethiopia. There was the story of her uncle, who had been shot as communist during the days of fascism. There was the story of her brief marriage, and the sudden, shocking accident that had deprived her of her husband. There was the tale of the distant cousin who had become a prostitute in Rome and whom she had tried to rescue from a bordello in the face of a screaming, threatening madam.

Emma realised, rather to her astonishment, that nothing, or virtually nothing, had ever happened to her; that when she held the incidents of her own life — such as they were — against the events experienced by Signora Sabatino, there was virtually nothing to say. Life was due to begin, though, now that she had left the cocoon of that school.

They fell into a comfortable routine. In the evenings, she would make her way over to Signora Sabatino's house and sit with her in the kitchen as she prepared dinner. There was no electricity in that house, and they would sit in the soft light of the oil lamps and eat the pasta which had been boiled over the wood stove. Then, when the meal was over and pots and plates washed, Emma would make her way by torchlight back to the large house and take to her bed and read.

She wrote to her father: "Everything is going so well. The days pass so easily, and I realise that I haven't really done very much, but that doesn't matter, does it? Signora Sabatino cooks dinner every evening, and is making a good cook of me. You'll see next time you're out here. And I start a music course in Siena soon.

It's terribly expensive, I'm afraid, but you don't mind, do you? I'm happy, Dad, I really am. But I will come back, sooner or later, don't worry about that . . ."

She went on the walk to the deserted church, and each time she went she put a coin in the charity box. Then she would go up the vineyards before turning and making her way back to the house. When she saw people in the vineyards, they recognised her now, and waved, and once or twice she spoke to them.

Then, one morning, she was on her walk, at a point just before the track reached the church, when she saw a movement off to one side. She stopped, thinking perhaps it was one of the oxen which grazed on the hillside, but it was a man, a young man, who was sitting on a rock under a tree. He had lifted his face when she approached, and was looking at her.

She stood where she was for a few moments, surprised rather than afraid, but wondering what he was doing. There was a farmhouse quite close by, a comfortable rather messy place, and she assumed that he lived there. He rose to his feet and began to walk towards her. When he was still some way off, he lifted a hand in greeting and called out to her, at first something that she did not catch, but then: "Where are you going?"

She looked at him. Now that he was close to her, she was struck by his extraordinary appearance. He was tall, but not at all awkward. His face, which was tanned olive by the sun, had the soft, glowing beauty of bright eyes and high forehead. He was, she thought, a young man from one of the Cinquecento paintings she had seen in Siena, the young man prepared for battle, body sculpted in strength, half way between boyhood and manhood.

"I'm on a walk," she said. "I walk over there every day."

She pointed towards the church, and he smiled.

"I think I've seen you before," he said. "You live down there, don't you?"

She nodded. "At the moment."

There was a silence between them, and she heard her heart beat within her. It seemed as if all her senses were charged with some curious electricity; and that she wanted nothing more than for this moment of contact to be prolonged.

"Where do you live?" she asked. "Do you come from that farm?"

He smiled. "Not quite, but I live around here, yes."

She looked at him, seized by a sudden, exhilarating recklessness.

"I was going to have a picnic tomorrow," she said, adding, rather lamely: "Since it's

Sunday. Would you like to join me?"

He appeared to think for a moment, and she felt an awful disappointment at the thought that he would say no, but he accepted her invitation.

"Let's meet here tomorrow," he said. "We can go and have our picnic in the vineyard. Would you like that?"

"I'll see you then," she said, and as she spoke, he turned away and went back towards the rock and the tree. She continued her walk, and when she came back there was no sign of him at all. As she approached the house she ran, skipping with sheer pleasure and excitement. She felt intoxicated, and sat down and said to herself: "Calm down. This is nothing special. You've met boys before."

But the truth of the matter was that she had never met a boy like that, and his insistent beauty, his grace, his extraordinary presence had burned into her very soul and seared it raw.

She telephoned her father, on a crackling, distant line, but did not tell him about the boy, or the picnic.

"You sound very cheerful," he said; and she pictured him suddenly, in his lonely house in the wasted light of London. "What's going on? What's happening out there?"

She found it easy to lie, because the lie was strictly true:

"Nothing's happening. I went for a walk to the church today."

"You put in a coin for me, I hope?"

"Of course."

"Good."

They spoke for a while longer and then hung up. She switched out the lights downstairs and went up to her room, alone in the empty house, but unafraid.

She packed the picnic basket carefully. She took filled rolls, and a fruit tart which she and Signora Sabatino had made that Friday, and wine — a bottle of chilled white wine tucked into a special vacuum sleeve to keep it cool. There was chocolate too, fruit, and *panforte di Siena,* which she had never been able to resist. Then she put the picnic basket on the back of her bicycle, secured it to the carrier, and set off for their rendezvous.

He was not there at first, which did not surprise her, as she realised that she was early. So she leant the bicycle against a tree and walked over to the small grove of olive trees that grew on the slope directly below the church. The grass there was dry and brittle from the summer heat, but there was shade where they might sit and the place was quite private.

She waited, glancing anxiously at her watch from time to time. Now he was late, and he would not be coming — she was sure of it. It had been a hare-brained idea anyway — a picnic with a boy whom she had met once and whose name she didn't even know: it was absurd. Of course he would not come.

But he did. Suddenly she looked up and saw him, walking over the grass towards her, and her heart gave a leap. He did not apologise for being late, but lowered himself to the ground, next to the picnic basket, and smiled at her. She reached for the basket, took out the wine and poured two glasses of the delicate, cool liquid. She handed him a glass, and he looked at it curiously, as if he was not accustomed to it, which could not be true, not here, amidst the vines.

He raised his glass to his lips, and sipped at it, frowning slightly as he did so.

She studied his face. He was as she had remembered him from the previous day — even more beautiful perhaps. There was a light about him, a chiaroscuro, and with each movement of his hands, or limbs, he seemed to diffuse that light.

She refilled his glass, and hers too. Then she passed him one of the rolls, and he ate it solemnly, still saying nothing, though this did not matter. She passed him a pear, which he sliced neatly and ate with evident pleasure. She had a piece of *panforte,* but he looked at it suspiciously, and she did not press him.

Then he arose, put down his glass, and gestured for her to stand up. She did so, as if in a daze, and he took the few steps towards her, opened his arms, and took her to him.

255

She did not resist, but put her arms around his neck, against child-smooth skin, and held him. She felt the wind in her hair, and there was light, and more light; she was lifted into the air, but she could not see, as the light seemed to have blinded her.

He set her down, and she lay back, her eyes closed. Then, when she opened them, he was gone — although he had been with her only minutes — and the picnic things were strewn around as if disturbed by a strong wind. The glasses had tumbled, and were lying, unbroken, on the ground; the other picnic things were scattered about, upturned, resting at impossible angles.

She did not feel surprised that he was not there; in a way, it would have been more surprising had he remained. Nor did she feel abandoned or unhappy; she was too aware of an extraordinary feeling of peace and resolution. She picked up the detritus of the picnic, dusted off the glasses, and set to re-packing the picnic basket. Then she made her way to the bicycle, cast only the briefest of glances behind her, and began the ride home down the white track.

She went into the house and put the picnic basket on the large kitchen table. Then she went upstairs, stripped off her clothes, and stepped into a cool shower. Her skin was hot, and she let the cold water needle against it, taking off the dust, drawing out the fever.

She put on a towelling gown and went to lie down on her bed. She did not think about what had happened, but she knew, intuitively, that she had been vouchsafed a mystery; and she remembered only the wind, and the light that had seemed to be all around them.

She did not leave the house for the next few days. Signora Sabatino came over to see that all was well, and went away reassured. She read, and sat under the pergola, dreaming. There were letters to write — letters begun, but not finished, and she busied herself with these. But she abandoned them, unable to talk about the one thing which possessed her. How could she? How could she describe the encounter?

Finally, a week or so later, she walked over to Signora Sabatino's house and asked her whether she could join her for supper that evening.

"Of course. We'll make a special meal together. You come."

And so she left the house, at dusk, and entered the comfortable ancient kitchen of Signora Sabatino's house, where the wood fire was glowing in the range, and where she felt so completely secure. They sat and talked, but her heart was not in their desultory, ordinary conversation, so that in a way it was a relief for her to be able to say:

"I went for a picnic. There was a boy

there, with me, a boy I had asked to come with me."

Signora Sabatino looked up from her pastry board.

"Who was he?"

"I don't know."

"You don't know?"

"No."

Then she added: "Something happened — I don't quite know what. I . . ."

Signora Sabatino looked at her, and knew, immediately.

"Where was it?" she asked. "How did you meet this boy?"

She told her, and then, at the end of the explanation, waited for the words of warning, of condemnation. But there were none — only, gravely, the measured words: "There are angels in those parts, you know. There always have been. My mother sometimes saw them — my uncles too. You are very fortunate. This boy you came across was an angel, don't you see? Do you realise that? An angel!"

She was curiously unsurprised by the revelation, largely because she had suspected that, or something like that. Signora Sabatino was right — of course there were angels in Italy, as there always had been. There were paintings to prove it — a whole iconography of angels in that classical Tuscan countryside — the angels of Botticelli, of Fra Angelico. They were there in the sky, on great wings as white as noon heat, on feathered pinions; they were there, in choirs, against the storm clouds, messengers militant; the bright squadrons. There was nothing untoward about meeting an angel, as Signora Sabatino seemed to understand. It may be unusual in other places, but here, there seemed nothing extraordinary about it.

Then, a short time later she knew that she was pregnant. She did not feel ill — in fact quite the opposite — and it was her extraordinary feeling of well-being, of lightness, that made her suspect her condition. Shortly afterwards, nature provided confirmation, and she took the bus into Siena and purchased, from a chemist shop near the Cathedral, a small self-diagnosis kit. The pharmacist who sold it to her — a woman — looked at her in pity, hesitated and then asked in hushed tones: "Do you need anybody to help you? There are nuns, you know. They will take in . . ." She paused; a man had come into the shop and was inspecting a toothbrush.

"Thank you. I am quite all right."

"I was only asking. I meant no offence."

"Thank you. I know."

The colours changed, as the instructions said they might, and she sat down on the edge of the bath and looked through the small window, out over the valley, to the hills beyond. She felt detached, as if the information was about somebody else. In a way, it had nothing to do with her at all; it had happened to her, in the same way as one might be struck by lightning, or chosen in a lottery; or afflicted with the misfortune of an illness. She had done nothing — nothing — and now she was expecting a baby.

In other circumstances, she would by now have faced, coldly and rationally, the options open to her. She would have gone to a doctor — of course she would — and have done what everyone did these days. It was her right, was it not? More than that, it was the right thing to do. She had her life before her — her course at university, everything — and there was no room for a baby, at least not yet. Accidents could be dealt with, clinically, discreetly.

But it was not like that now. There had been no mistake, no regretted moment of rash intimacy. She had been chosen, singled out; it was an annunciation. She would remain pregnant, she would have the baby, here in Italy. And then? She would keep the baby. She could not give away a gift such as that, an angel child.

Signora Sabatino had to know, and it was not difficult to tell her. The old woman sat silent for a moment, and then she rose and embraced her, weeping, stroking her hair, muttering to her words that she did not grasp.

Then: "I shall look after you. I shall move into the big house. That will be better."

She did not argue.

"I will make sure that everything is ready for the baby. I will fetch the midwife — there is a woman nearby who can look after all that. I will invite her some days before."

She felt herself absorbed by the plan, taken over by a female freemasonry of women and childbirth. This was nothing to do with men; this was an affair that was just for women. And this knowledge was reassuring. These women would not ask questions; they were concerned only for her and for the baby.

"Do not tell anybody about the father," she found herself asking. "Let others think he was just an ordinary boy."

Signora Sabatino nodded, holding a finger to her lips in a gesture of silence.

"It is not right to talk about angels," she said. "They are shy, and talk would frighten them off. But the father will probably come to see his child. He will know."

The next week, she resumed her walks to the church and the vineyard. She felt no anxiety, as she did not expect to see him. She stopped at the church, slipping the coin into its abyss, and then retraced her steps down the hill. She saw the place where they had sat for their picnic, but she did not approach it; nor did she linger outside the farm where she had at first thought he might live.

In the afternoons, she lay in her bedroom, in the cool, and read. Only later, when the sun was almost behind the hills, would she come downstairs and speak to Signora Sabatino, or sit outside and listen to the screech of the cicadas. She was aware of the child now; she sensed its fluttering movements within her, and she was thrilled by the feeling. She invited Signora Sabatino to place a hand against her stomach, and when the old woman felt the movements she crossed herself rapidly.

The months passed easily. By October, she was beginning to feel slow and heavy, and she donned the shifts which Signora Sabatino had made for her. She had gone to see a doctor, on Signora Sabatino's insistence, and she had examined her carefully, prodding at the child, who kicked back, making her smile. Everything was in order, she was told, but she might wish to have some tests. Abnormalities could be so easily detected. She listened, passively; they could test her if they wished, but they would never guess, with all their scientific sophistication, how this child had been conceived.

Signora Sabatino went with her to the hospital in Siena. They sat, mutely, on a bench before she was called into a sterile white room where they dressed her in a loose robe and then placed her on a table. Instruments were wheeled in, and there were explanations, but she paid little attention. And then, suddenly, they showed her the child on a screen, a small, confusing circle, which pulsated before her.

A doctor peered at the screen, and left the room. He returned, with several other doctors, who looked carefully at the image and spoke to one another under their breath. Then they performed other tests. She was placed before an X-ray screen and told to stand this way and that, while the doctors strained their eyes and pointed.

At the end of it all, with Signora Sabatino beside her, they broke the news. They did it gently, and one of the doctors touched her arm lightly as he spoke.

"We're terribly sorry," he said. "It will be very disappointing to you, but we think that your baby is deformed."

She said nothing, but Signora Sabatino spoke angrily.

"There is something on its back," one of them said. "We cannot really tell exactly, but there is some sort of growth. These things happen. And we think that you must now very carefully consider bringing this pregnancy to an end, even if it is rather late."

They looked at her expectantly. She glanced at Signora Sabatino, whose eyes had narrowed. Then the old woman leant forward to tell her something.

"This is what one might expect," she whispered. "It is an angel child, remember. It has wings. But don't tell them. They wouldn't understand. Let's just leave."

She nodded her agreement.

"Thank you," she said, turning to the doctors. "I will think about what you have told me."

She rose to her feet, and one of the doctors sprang forward to take her arm.

"You must not go just yet," he said. "You should stay. Then, tomorrow, when you have thought about it we can . . . we can arrange things."

She stared at him. The gown made her feel ridiculous, vulnerable, and it was hard to resist them. But she knew that she could not agree.

"No," she said. "I shall be going home now. Thank you."

She wrote to her father: "This is something which I find very difficult to say. All I ask of you is that you do not try to do anything about it. If you do, then I'm sorry but I shall have to go away somewhere. I mean that.

"I am expecting a baby in three months. I don't want to tell you how this happened, or who the father is. I ask you not to ask me about that, ever. If you love me, you'll accept this, and not say anything about it. I don't want you to try to get me to do anything; I don't want you to try to interfere in any way

264

at all with the arrangements I have made. In particular, don't phone me. If you want to see me, then come out here, but don't try to do anything. Nothing you do will change anything anyway."

She expected that the letter would take four days to reach him, and that he would appear on the fifth day. In fact, he came on the sixth, arriving in a rented car from Pisa Airport, streaked in dust from the drive. She watched him from her window as he parked the car outside, and carried his bag up the steps to the front door. She heard voices downstairs as he spoke to Signora Sabatino, and there was some shouting.

Then he was at her door, knocking perfunctorily before he turned the handle and came inside. Then he paused, and she saw that he was weeping, and that tears had run down from his face to make dark stains on his shirt front. She felt tender towards him, and ran across the room to embrace him.

"My darling," he sobbed. "My dearest. My girl."

"I'm all right, Dad. I'm fine — I really am."

"What happened? What happened to you? How did this thing . . ."

She placed her hand against his face, against the wet cheek.

"Nothing bad happened. I'm pregnant, that's all. It's not a big thing these days, you know."

He lowered his eyes.

"You should have told me before . . . much earlier."

"So I could have got rid of it?"

He lowered his eyes. "If necessary."

She looked at him carefully. "I'm keeping this baby. Do you understand that? I'm keeping the baby."

He turned away from her, dabbing at his eyes with a crumpled white handkerchief.

"I think you owe me some sort of explanation," he said, struggling to control his voice. "You can't just present me with this and say nothing about it!"

"What do you want to know?"

"Well, the father, of course. Who's the father? Where is he?"

"It doesn't matter," she said. "He's gone away. He's no longer here."

"His name? At least give me his name, for heaven's sake!" His voice was raised, full of misery, cracked with sorrow.

She looked at him glumly, and slowly the awful realisation dawned on him. His voice was quiet now, almost inaudible: "You don't know . . . You don't know, do you?"

She said nothing, but she took a step towards him as he seemed to crumple before her. Instinctively, he drew back, recoiling in horror, and she stood quite still, shocked at what she had done to him, at his pain.

He stayed for three days. They spoke about

it the next morning, when he accepted the conditions which she had stipulated in her letter.

"I won't ask you any more about it," he said. "But in return, please reassure me that you will never, never hesitate to come to me if you want to talk about it again. I will do anything for you, darling, anything. You know that, don't you?"

She ran towards him and flung her arms around him.

"I promise you," she whispered. "I promise."

"I have spoken to Signora Sabatino," he said, speaking slowly, as if the words were costing him pain. "And she told me one thing which has set my mind at rest. She tells me that you weren't . . . you weren't attacked. That's all that I really wanted to hear. I don't mind about the rest. It's just that — that one thing — that a father can't bear. Do you understand that?"

"Yes."

"So now we should discuss how I can help you. Are you sure you want to stay here? Are you sure you wouldn't like to come home?"

"I want to stay," she replied. "I really am happy here."

"Very well. What about a nurse? Can I arrange for a nurse to come, say, a few weeks before the baby's due?"

She shook her head. "Signora Sabatino's

looking after me. She's tremendous."

He looked doubtful. "She's getting on a bit . . ."

"She's fine."

There was silence for a few moments. "Where will you go? Will you have the baby in Siena?"

"Maybe," she said. "We'll see what the doctor suggests. There's a midwife apparently. She could come out here. I'd prefer that."

"You'll listen to what the doctor advises, though?" His voice was anxious, and she patted him on the back reassuringly.

"Of course, Dad. I'm not stupid."

Afterwards, they relaxed. She thought that he had come to terms with the situation now, and they talked about other matters. He promised to come out again, as soon as he could, as soon as his business would allow him, and she promised that she would telephone him every week. They parted fondly, and she stood in the driveway watching his car disappear down the road towards the town, waiting until it was no longer visible and she was an adult again.

In the last few weeks, she felt lazier and more passive. She had had an easy pregnancy, with little discomfort, and she found it difficult to imagine how this feeling of fulfilment could change so suddenly to pain. And when the first warning came, and she felt the jolt, even then it seemed to be sufficiently remote not to cause her distress. She called Signora Sabatino, who immediately hurried to the telephone to summon the midwife. Then she returned and led her to the bed, holding her hand as she lay there.

The midwife arrived and busied herself with preparations. She was a large woman, with sleeves rolled up to reveal thick, masculine arms. She applied a sharp-smelling liquid to her hands and arms and measured Emma's pulse against a watch which she took out of her pocket. Then she asked for towels to be boiled and sat down on a chair beside the bed.

"I delivered a baby in this house once before," she said. "It was a long time ago. It was a very large baby."

She closed her eyes. The pain was returning, the fire that was licking at her body; but she was not afraid. The light had come back; she could feel it; and it was all about her. It overcame the tearing of the flesh; the agony. The light.

And then, the fire rose to a great roar, and the light was almost too bright to bear, and she heard the cry. The midwife was back at her side, and Signora Sabatino was behind her. There was a white bundle, and another cry, and she saw Signora Sabatino bend down, take the bundle from the midwife, and pass it to her, into her arms.

"A boy," said Signora Sabatino. "Your little boy! *Eccolo!*"

She held the child, and saw its wrinkled face and the eyes, now open, trying to focus. She wept, and the midwife passed a cloth across her cheek.

"Well done," she said. "Brave girl. Brave girl."

Then she reached into the wrappings of towels and exposed the baby's body, the skin in tiny folds, so red. She felt the tiny limbs, which moved under her touch, and her hand went to his back. There were two slight bulges, smooth to the touch, but wet, as if moist skin had been folded against skin. She looked up at Signora Sabatino, who had come between her and the midwife.

"Yes," whispered the old woman. "He has them. He has the wings of an angel."

She dressed him in gold, in the robes made for him by Signora Sabatino; for his father would come soon, she felt, and he must be appropriately attired. The child, who had slept so silently for the first three days of his life, who had woken only to suckle, now lay in his crib, with the two women about him, one on her bed, the other in a chair, sewing.

He came in the evening. Suddenly there was a light outside, and the sound of wind. Signora Sabatino rose wordlessly to open the door and he entered the room. He, too, was in robes of gold, a light blue belt about his waist. She turned her face to him and smiled, and he came towards her and held out a hand to her cheek. Then, without saying anything, he walked to the crib and took the child into his arms. Signora Sabatino had dropped to her knees now, and had reached out to touch the hem of his robe as he walked past.

Two other angels entered, two women, in dresses of silver. He passed the child to one of them and then he turned to face the mother.

"You will see him again one day," he said. "He will not be far away."

She nodded. "I know."

"You are not unhappy?"

"No, I am not."

He gestured to the two angels in silver, and then he himself moved towards the door. For a moment he hesitated, as if he wished to say more, but then he stepped out. For a while there was still light, both in the room and without, but this soon faded, and the night returned.

ABOUT THE AUTHOR

ALEXANDER MCCALL SMITH is the author of over fifty books, including the *No. 1 Ladies' Detective Agency* series of novels, which has sold over 2.5 million copies in the US alone and has been translated into twenty-six foreign languages. In 2003 he was the winner of the UK's principal award for humorous writing, the Saga Award, and in the same year he won the Glenfiddich Award for Writing. Alexander McCall Smith lives in Scotland.

MG
1/05